CONTENTS

CHAPTER 1

"I understand what you're saying, Mr. Foxx, but I simply cannot continue to allow you to skip years every time you ask me! It just isn't fair to the other students, many of whom have studied here for far longer then you have, nor is it fair to you." The Grand Master said, raising his hand to gesture around the room in frustration. "Have you even bothered to form connections with either your peers? Or the faculty for that matter?"

"I have friends, Sir. If that's what you're asking." Shifting my gaze away from the man's doubting grey eyes, I turned my attention to the many books and various items of interest around the office. I didn't understand what being social had to do with learning. Seemed more like a distraction, honestly.

"According to the various reports I've gotten about you, many of which express *concern*, I find this hard to believe." The older man sighed and followed my gaze as it traveled across the many hundreds of aged texts and miscellaneous trinkets. "Social connections are an important part of academia, Mr. Foxx. Both during your education and beyond."

Hearing the frustration in the man's voice, I finally tore my attention from a section of the wall and the various books on it. Some of them had titles I had never heard of and I wondered if I might borrow them. Feeling grey eyes bore into me, I finally looked at the older Mage. From his appearance alone he didn't seem like much. Middle-aged, approaching his fifty-seventh year, with graying black hair and a neatly trimmed beard. He was well dressed, as a man of his position should be, and had a face lined with signs of stress and exhaustion. Part of me felt bad for coming to him with my complaints, but I dismissed it. *That's his job. He should be used to for it.*

"I understand, Sir. I just feel that it is a waste of my talents to be studying subjects that I already understand. I don't believe my current professors have the ability to teach me any further." I could tell from the thinning of his mouth that he didn't appreciate my dismissal of his staff's abilities. "Not to say that they aren't masters of their fields – I'm certain they are – but the subjects they're teaching...bore me."

I cringed inwardly, knowing that I had sounded more like a child than a grown man, but held my ground and kept the man's gaze. It was the truth, and nothing would change it. I was bored and felt like I was being stagnated by the educators I had.

The man trained his gray eyes on me, and rubbed his neatly bearded chin, scratching at a small patch of white hair. After a while he sighed and leaned back in his dark, red-leather chair, tapping his fingers on the surface of his desk. "Richard, your ability to grasp magic is extraordinary. Beyond anything I have ever seen in my decades of teaching. Truly it is a remarkable gift, and I am sorry you feel you are not being challenged in your studies."

Sighing in relief, I lean forwards, "Thank you, Grand Master!"

"Allow me to finish, please." Lowering his hand, which had been raised to stop me from speaking further, the Grand Master gestured around him. "I felt the same way you do when I was a young man. Not to the same degree, I would wager, but similar enough. The complexity of the courses is not geared towards a Mage of your gifts. A common issue with generalized learning, I'm afraid."

The man pauses before gesturing to me, his lips taking a slight downwards tilt. "I cannot, however, continue to allow you to skip forward. Your knowledge and control may exceed the level of your peers, but your impulsiveness and lack of social connections worry me. I have seen many men and women fall apart after moving too far, too fast."

Grimacing as he finished his explanation, I slumped in my own dark red leather chair. Doing my best to withhold a sigh of frustration as I considered his words carefully before shaking my head and lifting my gaze to meet his. "Sir, please. It feels like I'm getting nowhere, and it is frustrating. Surely I can do *something*? I'll do anything! Just let me skip ahead one more year, just one!"

"No, Mr. Foxx. I don't think that is in your best interest. My duty as the Grand Master of this university entails more than just your academic performance. I need to watch out for your mental and social well-being as well." Leaning back in his chair and turning his gaze to the ceiling in consideration, the older Mage tapped his fingers together. "Have you considered maybe that you're approaching your education here in the wrong way?"

"Sir?" I tilted my head in confusion. "The wrong way?"

"Yes. You're so focused on mastering the courses provided that you're not looking *outside* them for materials that interest you. You're tunnel-visioning your education." Gesturing around him, the man continued. "You showed interest in the many tomes and scrolls in my office, yes? Why not examine them closer and tell me what you discover."

Furrowing my brow in confusion, I push my chair back from my side of his desk and make my way around the room to do as he asked. Coming to the first of many texts, I noted that it was dedicated to fire magics, specifically, on their construction in environments that aren't suited for flame. The texts to its left detailing the subject further, focusing on specific environments like the southern rain forests, the arctic north, and even underwater. *A series? I wonder if I can borrow these...*

A quick glance showed that the author of the texts was the same individual – one Tellan Norn – I continued to browse the shelves. As I explored, I started to see a pattern and by the eighth text I had come realize what he was trying to show me. "These are all the same subject matter, aren't they? Most of them, at least. Elemental Magic and their theory and application."

"Indeed, Mr. Foxx. Can you remember what my Mastery was in?" The Grand Master said, genuine curiosity in his voice.

"Yes, you mentioned it in your introduction during my first year. Ulirk Tyam, you obtained an Elemental Magic Mastery two and a half decades ago while studying here." The memory was enough easy to recall, as was what came after his introduction. "You put on quite the demonstration. I believe Professor Daylin called it "beyond risky and foolish," if memory serves."

At the mention of the, rather infamous, tongue lashing the Grand Master had received from the Alchemy professor, the older man waved his hand in dismissal. "Do you understand what I am suggesting here, Mr. Foxx?"

"I believe so, Sir." Letting the man change the subject, I turned my attention back to the shelves I had been exploring before. Tracing the bindings of one of the newer tomes, written by the Grand Master himself, I gave the obvious answer. "You want me to pursue a Mastery, Sir? Wouldn't that be tunnel-visioning, as you called it?"

"Not necessarily. Please, sit and let me explain." Turning to look at the man, who gestured me back over to the desk, I made my way back to my seat. Once I was situated, he reached over to small side desk and grabbed the handle of a silver kettle, lifting it from a metal tray. "Tea?"

"No, Sir, thank you." Shaking my head at the offered drink, I waited patiently for the man to pour himself a generous cup of the hot drink. After adding sugar and milk to his drink, the older Mage leaned back in his seat and continued.

"In a matter of speaking, yes, a Mastery is a form of "tunnel-vison." Sipping from his drink, the Grand Master took a moment to savor it before looking back around the room. "But many Mages, including myself, choose to focus their attention on a sin-gular subject in their later years, as you know. This is what I sug-gest. Consider it a hobby with future benefits."

"So, you will encourage me to start on a Mastery early, but not allow me to skip a year in my general academics?" The logic had me confused, and I couldn't help but feel that the Grand Master was being slightly unfair. "Wouldn't it be better to just allow me to move ahead in my studies and place me with students that are doing the same?"

"There are no students doing the same, Mr. Foxx. Mastery is a self-driven pursuit with limited oversight from any professor. A far cry from the classroom-based studies you are familiar with." Reaching into his desk, the Grand Master dug around – pushing aside several objects and muttering to himself. "In most cases, you are assigned a specific instructor as a "guide" to the process, but I believe I can fill that role."

"I would be honored to have you as my guide, Sir. May I ask what you're looking for?" Watching the man with curiosity, I leaned forward to try and catch a glimpse of some of the objects in the drawer. Due to the poor angle, I could only see an ink pot and several pieces of parchment.

"Just a little something that might assist you in your new studies – Ah! Here it is." Removing his hand from the desk, the man closed the drawer and offered me a pin. It was a simple thing, an iron book with a large rune engraved on its front, but any student at the university would recognize it.

"Sir? Are you certain?" Reaching out to take the offered object, I looked it over in poorly disguised shock – knowing its implications. "I mean, I will gladly take it, but I want to make sure you're not making a mistake…"

"Yes, I'm sure. Unrestricted access to the library, and the tens of thousands of tomes that lie within it. Find something that interests you, Mr. Foxx. And do be careful, some things are beyond even your understanding. I trust my faith in you will not be misplaced?" I felt a compulsion to raise my eyes to meet the piercing gaze of the Grand Master. His grey eyes burning through my brown ones, seeking…something.

"No, Sir. I won't abuse this gift you've given me." Shaking my head, tearing my gaze from his, I pinned the iron book to the front of my robes. "I promise."

"Good. Make sure you don't lose that pin and come to me if you have questions or concerns regarding your studies – specifically your Mastery. My door is *always* open to you, Mr. Foxx." Nodding at the man's words, and knowing a dismissal when I hear one, I reach across the desk to shake his hand and made my way to the door. Turning to bow my head in respect before slipping out of the large office.

Making my down the halls of the administration building, where the Grand Master and those that ran the university's schools of magic worked, I decided to take the long way towards the dormitory. Taking a right at the waiting room near the front of the building to exit near the grand fountains that were situated at the university's heart. It was a massive pool of water, easily several dozen yards in width, with towering statues placed throughout. Each statue had some relation to either the university or the city that surrounded it, being a notable individual or even entity. Several dozen students, encompassing various levels of study, sat around the giant decoration. Some reading, some practicing the various small-scale magics we could use outside of designated areas. Simple things such as moving the water of the fountain, creating small balls of light or flame, or forming a shield around yourself and your books to avoid getting them wet from the ever-present mist.

Making my way around the large pool of water and the dozen or so statues found within it I took a right at a forked pathway. The students surrounding the pool barely paying me any mind as I walked past them, though a few that shared classes with me at some point did give a small nod in greeting. As I walked down the path that would take me towards the dormitory and away from the campus proper, I heard the students cheer and the fountain grow in volume. A clear sign that the Enchantment on the decoration had activated, as it does every hour.

Turning to watching the gigantic statues move across the water, performing an elegant mix of dance and battle, I admired the strength of the Enchantment. *Surprised that it's still going after all these years. Must be recharged yearly, no other way.*

The Enchantment in question had been created by a Grand Master of years past to entertain guests and students alike. Considering the size of the spell, it would have taken an immense level of skill and dedication. Likely a Mastery of the subject. *A Mastery of Enchantment. Would I like something like that?*

Shaking my head to dismiss the thoughts, I watched as a giant wolf statue, a representation of the mortal-turned-god, Drakari, ended the show. Lifting its head and giving a silent howl as water erupted from its mouth like a geyser. The show over, I continued my walk to the dorms. Absent-mindedly casting a more advanced barrier charm on myself compared to the other students. The statues had a small tendency to target those with weaker barriers, sending strong waterspouts at them.

An immensely powerful Enchantment charm, one that took likely years to perfect, and its used as a practical joke. A practical joke that had led to many students, and even guests, being soaked and bitter.

A shriek of outrage as I turned made it to the end of my chosen path let me know that the statues had, once again, struck. Finding a target, likely a first-year student, that wasn't prepared. Shaking my head with a sigh, I took a turn and made my way down towards the southern half of the campus. It was there that the dormitories and dining hall were located.

Along the way, I noted many dejected looking students. They were sitting on benches and railings, head in their hands and looking panicked. Likely, these were the ones that had failed the yearly exams that took place to determine your scholarship eligibility. No doubt, these same students would be forced to return home at the end of the term and face their parent's disappointment. *Should have studied more, idiots.*

Some of the most legendary magic users in history have studied at this school, and many more have taught here over the course of its existence. It is a privilege to attend it, even if for only a year's time, and many would kill for the chance. Tuition alone is a king's ransom. If you do not take it seriously, and commit all your energy and time to studying, you should make room for those that can. *Unless you're a student with particularly large purse-strings...*

"Hey! Richard! Richard over here!" Turning to look in the direction of the voice that called to me, I caught sight of my roommate and somewhat friend, Tristifer. The blonde-haired youth running towards me from what I guessed was the dining hall. "Richard! I'm so happy to see you!"

*Speaking of said students...*I sighed and looked the other man over, taking in the slight flush of his cheeks and the way he played with his collar. Narrowing my eyes, I quickly deduced what he wanted. "Did you lock yourself out of our room again?"

"No! Well, maybe? I didn't cast the spell that did it, if that's what you're asking! It was just...there when I got back." The other man kicked at the ground sheepishly, brushing off imaginary dust from his. Looking me over, likely trying to find a way to change the subject, he caught sight of my new pin. "No way! Is that what I think it is?! Where did you get it?!"

"From the Grand Master, of course. Where did you think I was for the last hour or so?" Brushing off his attention, I returned to the more important question – the locking of our room. "Who locked the door, Tristifer? What happened?"

"Selena." He meekly replied, diverting his gaze to the stone pathway beneath our feet. It took me a moment to recognize the name as the girl he was currently pursuing *romantic relations* with. Or, had been, I guess.

"You two broke up?" I asked, gesturing for the other man to follow me. Forgoing my longer walk in order to get back to the dormitory and solve the problem as quickly as possible. *She better not have touched my belongings.*

"Not...exactly?" Tristifer said, quickly moving to walk beside me. "We're taking a break from each other – seeing other people. It's complicated."

"Oh, of course." I rolled my eyes, giving a small noise of disbelief. "So, you broke up *temporarily.*"

He had nothing to say to this, of course, and so chose to remain quiet. He knew that I had nothing but distaste for his seemingly endless *romantic pursuits* on campus, having had four girlfriends this year alone. This was especially true when they inevitably impacted me by proxy. I decided to drop the subject for the moment and continue our trek to the dormitory in silence, ending any of his attempts to start up a new conversation with a sharp glare.

Arriving at the dormitory I take a moment to admire the white marble building and its ancient architecture. It was, like many of the older buildings on the campus, built in the same imposing and awe-inspiring style. Large stained-glass windows that showcased various religious scenes related to the Church of Drakari as well as twelve tall spires that were divided into two groups of size by a massive dome at the center. The spires and dome were supposed to signify the twelve Elder Gods and the ascension of Drakari to the High Seat after the wolf's self-sacrifice and subsequent rise to godhood.

The fact that many of the buildings on campus were designed in such a way was no surprise, given that the university was, and still is to some degree, a religious institute. Only the Church has moved to the other end of campus to newer and more grandiose buildings. The price for such constructions, and their maintenance, was, of course, added to the cost of tuition.

Shaking my head, remembering the outrageous price of attendance, I pushed open one of the dormitory's massive wooden doors. Making my way to the Enchanted lifts just beyond them and pressing the rune that would call it too my level. They were magical constructs, likely created by the same Grand Master that Enchanted the fountain and were found in many of the buildings on campus. Hearing footsteps behind me, I turned and glared at Tristifer.

"You're taking the stairs. Consider it a punishment." Pointing to the stone steps just behind him, I made sure to keep my glare on the blond to accent my point.

At first, I though the man would protest, or at least make some sort of fuss, but after a moment he merely sighed and nodded. "That's fair. I'll meet you up there, then."

Pressing the rune that symbolized our floor – the third, and last – I watched the other student make his way up the first of six staircases he would have to endure. The building was large, after all, and each floor was tall. *At least I'll have a moment to work on the lock in peace.*

Sighing at the situation, I ignored the odd feeling in my stomach and chest as the lift rose upwards. My mind drifting to the subject I would pick for my Master. *Enchanting has many applications, and it's complex. It could be enjoyable to study.*

I'd never considered studying Enchantment, or at least not as a sole focus. When I'd first encountered these lifts two years ago, I had been amazed by them and the spells they utilized. The same with the fountain at the center of the university. That amazement had died down as time wore on, and they'd become just another aspect of life on campus. *Would the same happen if I studied Enchantment? Would I lose interest in it as time went on?*

My thoughts were interrupted at the small "ding" that alerted me to my arrival at my chosen floor, causing me to shake my head and push my musings to the back of my mind. Stepping off the lift and glancing towards the stairs to see no sign of Tristifer yet, I made my way to our dorm room. It was the third door from the staircase, a simple dark wooden barrier set in a stone frame and worn from several years of use. Our names two last names, Foxx and Dale, etched into a bronze plaque that had been nailed to the door itself.

Turning my attention to the similarly bronze door handle and lock, I frowned at the pieces of metal. The lighting in the dormitory was good, at least. Provided by smokeless, magical torches, and so it was easy to see the small rune engraved at the point where the handle met the door. Another Enchantment. Part of me wondered if this was a sign from the Gods that I should choose the field of study. *They could have chosen a better way to do it than this minor annoyance.*

Rolling my eyes and gesturing to the door I activated what students of magic *creatively* call "The Mage Sight." Magic, as an energy force, is not typically visible to the naked eye. It is unseeable to the untrained, requiring a great deal understanding, study, and a natural talent in order to perceive and utilize it. One in a hundred will have access to it in some capacity, but only a scarce few will have real talent or potential to cast spells or do anything impressive. Control, Will, Skill, and Faith, the most important components of a spell. The last being why a Church would be associated with a magical university.

The Mage Sight, or The Sight as it was sometimes called, allows a magic user to see spells, their own or another's. Magic, to users of The Sight, appears as a "weave" of power and Will, intent in most cases. The weave's complexity was determined by the Skill of the user, of course. Tristifer's scorned lover, and I have no doubt he was the one to scorn her, had the desire to lock the door, so her Will and power have taken that intent and centralized it around the door and its handle. Her Skill makes this weave rather complex, certainly beyond Tristifer's capabilities, and her Faith that the weave will hold overpowers his own Faith in his abilities.

Does that mean that Tristifer isn't confident about his skills as a Mage? It certainly didn't seem like it, given my interaction with the blond. *Surely, he could undo a weave as simple as this.*

"What do you think, Richard? Can you undo it? Should I get a professor?" The voice of my roommate broke me from my thoughts. I turned, my Sight still active, to look at the anxious face of Tristifer.

"No, I can do it. While this might be complicated for someone of *your* capabilities, your girlfriend's spell isn't all that impressive." Ignoring his response to me questioning his abilities, which were, admittedly, not too terrible, though I'll never say so out loud, I turned my gaze back to the lock. "She's made quite a few mistakes in her haste. Likely because she was so angry."

Which, again, is why I'm surprised Tristifer couldn't handle the weave himself. *Why do I care?*

Dismissing the thoughts and sharpening my focus, I turned my Sight to one of the weave's mistakes. Tearing through Selena's spell easily with a sharp exertion of my Will, the locking spell fell apart into nothingness. Its power dissipating into the air harmlessly. Reaching out to tentatively prod at the door with my magic, checking for any additional surprises. I nodded at Tristifer that it was all clear.

"You sure?" Tristifer asked, nervously looking at the door handle and then to me. "Not that I'm questioning your abilities, Richard, it's just…"

Sighing at his hesitance, I reached out and grabbed the door handle while staring at him in annoyance. Seeing his apologetic look, I rolled my eyes and opened the door, noting with a grimace that the locking mechanism was destroyed. Pieces of it falling out of the door to the floor. Not only that but the handle was a little too loose, Selena's last parting gift, I suppose.

"We'll have to alert the campus about this so they can have it repaired." I stood, sighing at the ruined door.

"I'll send in a request. I'm sorry, Richard. I'll try to be more careful from now on." Turning a doubtful look in the other student's direction, I shook my head and entered our room. Noting that it appeared as we'd left it earlier in the day, meaning that Selena hadn't tampered with our belongings. *I hope.*

Still, I kept my Sight activated as I made my way into the room, looking over anything that was out in the open with caution. Something that Tristifer seemed to notice as he activated his own Sight before entering the room. Slowly making his way to his side and prodding his possessions. Finding nothing out of the ordinary on my side, I made my way over to my travel bag and began to load it up with various studying supplies from my desk.

"You going somewhere, Richard?" Tristifer asked, siting on his bed and watching me with interest.

"The library." Picking up one of my journals and flipping through it, I was annoyed to see that half of it had been filled up already. "There's something I want to look up."

"Does it have anything to do with the Master pin on your chest?" My roommate tried to ask casually, but I could detect the jealousy in his voice.

"Maybe." Receiving a look of annoyance at my vague answers, I sighed and decided to give the blond more to go on. "The Grand Master gave me something to look into. To help me with my studies, that is."

At my words, the other student furrowed his brow. Looking at me in consideration I could see that he'd already gathered the gist of what this all meant. Tristifer, despite my dislike of some of his *activities* was *not* a dull man. He wasn't a mental giant, though few at the university where, in my opinion, but he wasn't *slow.* "You're studying for your Mastery, aren't you? Are you really that far ahead?"

"No. Well, I don't think so? I'm not sure *when* one studies for a Mastery, honestly. According to the Grand Master, it just happens when a student, or more importantly, a professor thinks that they're ready." Finding a journal with adequate space for new notes and making a note to purchase a new set, I packed away a few ink pots and a good pen before standing up right.

"More like you badgered him about advancing another year and this was his solution." Tristifer snorted with laughter, moving to lay on his bed and stare at his ceiling in consideration. Rolling my eyes at him, ignoring the flush of embarrassment that he was right, I made my way to the door.

"Hey, Richard?" Tristifer started suddenly, causing me to look back at him. The blond was still staring at the ceiling in thought, a small frown on his face. "Be careful, alright? I know you're smart and all but…"

The sudden concern caught me off guard, as but I dismissed it with a shrug and turned back to the door. Pulling it open with ease due to its broken state, I looked back over my shoulder. "Don't worry about me. Just get our door fixed, ok?"

Not waiting for his response, I exited our dorm room and shut the door behind me. Making my way to the lifts again and pressing the rune that summoned, I pondered Tristifer's concern as well as the Grand Master's warning. *They act like I'm going to go and do something foolish! It's just studying for a Mastery, it's not that complicated or dangerous.*

Entering the lift when it arrived, I made my way down the brief trip to the ground floor, once more ignoring the odd sensations that happened as the magical device moved. Exiting the lift's small confines and walking to the large doors, I pressed my hand against one to shove it open. As I did so, my eyes drifted upward for a moment to and caught piercing gold. The glare of a wolf, rising from bright light and surrounded by twelve white figures, held me in place. For a moment, I felt uncertainty fill me. But, as quick as it came, it passed, and I shook my head.

Now they're getting to me, too! Scowling and pushing the door open harshly, I briskly walked in the direction of the library. The memory of those golden eyes and the feelings they invoked pushed to the back of my mind.

CHAPTER 2

Making my way across the campus, I made sure to keep an eye on my peers as they passed me. Magic had an odd effect on people, I'd found, especially on those that were bored and new to it. First year students at the university were particularly guilty of this. They delighted in showing off their prowess and skill. This was especially true in large, crowded areas such as the courtyard between the Medical Magic ward, the Combat Magic ward, and the library. The fact that one of the flashier schools of magic, Battle Magic, was taught near healers was not a coincidence.

More than one reckless first year student had, full of bravado and a false sense of superiority after their first Combat Magics class, issued a challenge to a passerby. Either wordlessly through a sudden spell, or by direct confrontation. It was an unspoken agreement that, willing or not, any students entering this space were free game for a duel of sorts.

I could see several of the students lift their heads from where they read, sitting on the various benches and rails throughout the area, and look at me as a potential target. Thankfully, the first years seemed to be rather tame today, and no one issued a challenge. Likely due to many them being culled by the latest scholarship exam. That said, I didn't lower my guard, or cease using the Mage Sight, for an instant. Keeping an eye out for any weaves that might form even as I made my way up the stone steps to the massive library's doors.

The library is only a few minutes' walk from the dormitories, which is convenient for students, and is the second largest structure on the campus. Beaten only by the recently constructed

Church of Drakari's cathedral-palace. Its, subsequently, the second largest building in the entirety of Libira, the city in which our university is located. Like many of the other buildings on campus that are particularly old the library is made of white stone and features large painted-glass windows. Unlike most of the other windows on campus, however, the library has a combination of both religious and magical scenes. Its doors are massive, able to fit four or five men, side by side, through them at once.

Thankfully, whatever material these barriers were made from is also extremely lightweight, allowing me to push one of the massive double doors open without much resistance. Entering the library quickly, shutting the door behind me, I sighed in relief that I hadn't received a last-minute prank from one of the students outside. Composing myself, I looked around the massive center of learning, admiring the sight like so many times before.

The first thing one would notice when entering is the large ring situated directly in the center of the first floor. This ring was composed from a combination of desks as well as tables and was where near two dozen Mages worked. Their robes a dark red, lined with white, and the symbol of the university sewn into the breast, a white wolf, resting on a stone slab. Around the ring are what appeared to be an endless maze of shelves, covered in what seemed like limitless books and scrolls.

These Mages are known as the Lorekeepers, individuals tasked with maintaining and tracking all the books and scrolls in the nearly 1300-year-old library. They take their job seriously, and any student that steps out of line is dealt with harshly. In some cases, their authority even supersedes that of the Grand Master, especially when it comes to the library. Senior students even say that the red-robed Mages can even issue expulsion on the spot. *Though, those are only rumors – no one's ever seen them expel a student.*

Rumors or not, the library's keepers had a fearsome reputation, one that even senior students were scared into submission by. The red robed figures paid me little mind outside a small glance in my direction as I approached the center ring, wordlessly delegating the task of dealing with me to one of the closest members, a middle-aged woman that looked near the Grand Master's age. Said woman gestured me over to her desk with a single finger, sliding a small stack of tomes to the side to see me better.

Approaching her, I tried to keep as confident as I could, even as her magic began to lock on to mine. Something I could see due to my Sight still being active. *Likely memorizing my magical signature or imprinting it on a magical tracker. I've heard rumors that they have such an Enchantment, though it was never confirmed...*

Not showing any discomfort at the prickling feeling of her magic washing over me, I waited patiently for her to finish. Feeling it center around the pin on my chest for a moment, then cease. "The Master's Section, I assume?"

"Yes, please." I said, nodding and touching the iron pin. Seeing her eyes glance to it before she returned the nod herself.

"Follow me." Standing and striding to the spiral staircase located directly behind the Lorekeeper's ring of desks, we walk up several flights of stairs before arriving at our destination. A locked gate that was sealed by magics so complex that I winced just looking at it.

The weave didn't seem to have an end, or even a beginning. Just an endless motion of magic, constantly whirling and changing. Every time I thought I had figured it out, it suddenly changed, leaving me back at the start. With this kind of Enchantment, I was not surprised that no one had ever successfully broken into the Master's section before.

"If you have any questions, please direct them to the Lorekeepers present on this floor. You will find them along the center railing, at their desks, or walking down the aisles. Have a pleasant day." With that said, the woman reached into her pocket and retrieved a small key, one that appeared to be made from the same materials as the gate. My Sight saw that it also featured an exceptional complicated weave, though apparently whirling in the opposite direction.

The moment the key slipped into the hole; my Sight allowed me to see the two weaves temporarily merge into one chaotic mess. Then, suddenly, both spells came to a halt. Forming a singular, perfect weave, solid and humming with energy as the seal that held the door closed unraveled and the barrier opened. Nodding at the Lorekeeper, I made my way through the doorway, which closed behind me. I didn't have to look back to know that the chaotic weave had returned the moment the key had been removed.

Turning my attention to what appears like endless rows of tomes and scrolls, and the sparse handful of individuals sitting among them, I felt overwhelmed. There was so much knowledge available, so many subjects to study, and I was to try and focus on only one of them?! *I'm starting to wonder if this was a gift or a punishment.*

The atmosphere of the Master's section didn't help, either. Each shelf was crafted from a dark wood, giving them a shadowy appearance. Even in the bright magical light provided by the smokeless torches throughout. Overall, the entire area was a labyrinth of knowledge, and turning my gaze upwards only amplified this feeling as I saw three *more* levels now accessible. Each likely filled with the same seemingly endless shelves.

Feeling overwhelmed, and not knowing where to even *begin* my pursuit of knowledge, I decided to do the one thing I rarely do. *I need help. Maybe one of the Lorekeepers can assist me?*

With that thought in mind, I take my first few tentative steps into the Master's section. Walking down the aisles, glancing at the subjects of some of the books as I do so, I try and find one of the library's caretakers. Passing by several older students I notice a cart filled with books and scrolls in the distance. Likely, one of the Lorekeepers was doing their duty and stocking the shelves. Approaching the cart, I was happy to see that I wouldn't have to wait long as one of the library's caretakers rounded the corner just as I arrived.

Whereas the Lorekeepers below the Master's Section wore red robes, this one wore dark purple and had the necklace awarded to graduates of the university around his neck. I also noted, without much surprise, that he had the same iron book pin as myself. As the guardians of the largest and greatest collection of ancient texts, I suppose it made sense that they would be both a Master and a graduate of the university. Clearing my throat and getting the man's attention, I gestured to the pin on my chest.

"Excuse me? I've been told to consider a topic for studying but don't really know where to start..." I tried to not come off as too sheepish or clueless but was certain that the man saw right through me.

The Lorekeeper looked me up and down, his hands sliding across the spines of the texts on his cart and hummed in thought. I could see magic brushing across each book and scroll in a pattern that I couldn't quite understand at my angle, but thought that it might have something to do with how the Lorekeepers categorize the library's contents. Gesturing for me to follow him, the Lorekeeper continued to attend to his task. Pulling the cart behind him as he walked.

"New to Mastery I take it? What year are you?" The Lorekeeper slipped one of the tomes on the cart into a seemingly random spot without looking at its spine, confirming my earlier assumption about it being a categorization spell.

"Fourth, though I've only been at the university for two years." My admission had him turning to look at me, slightly stunned. The expression faded from his face however and he shook his head with a small laugh.

"No wonder you're confused! You probably have no idea what the hells you want to do. Just followed the standard courses I take it, maybe some of the more intermediate subjects?" Seeing my nod, he hummed in thought and placed another book. "What are you looking for, exactly?"

"Well, a Mastery is something I'll dedicate a large portion of my life to, they say. So, I'd like it to be something that's at least complex, with many variables. I'd thought about Enchantment, or maybe Alchemy, but..." I shrugged and he nodded in consideration, eyes lighting up as he turned his attention back to the cart behind him. This time he looked at the spines of the books, muttering to himself before picking one up and handing it to me.

"Those two would be excellent choices based on your criteria, but they're far from the only option available to you. There's one other path you could take." Seeing my questioning look, he gestured to the book he had handed to me.

Giving him a confused glance, I turned to the cover of the text and furrowed my brow. "Conjuration? Isn't that just an advanced form of Transfiguration?"

"Oh, aye. It can be perceived as that. But there's much more to it than that. Much, much more. You need to know the ins and outs of all the things you're trying to Conjure, the way magic flows in the weave, and much more. Not only that, but you have to do it all quickly." Seeing he had my attention, he gestured to the book in my hand. "Why don't you read that and tell me what you think?"

Taking a moment to look over the book and considering his words, and what little I knew about the subject off-hand, I bit my lip in consideration. Like Enchanting and Alchemy, it sounded like a great idea. Maybe even perfect given that it required me to think on my feet rather than slowly, like Alchemy and Enchanting. Those subjects weren't too fast paced, with some projects even capable of being worked on for days, if not weeks.

"Is Conjuration challenging? Something that stands out, that is." I asked suddenly, turning my full attention to the Lorekeeper.

My question caught him off guard, but he nodded slowly. "Yes, I'd say so. Master's of the subject are rare due to its complexity. There are only a few books in the entire library dedicated to it, in fact. Most seem to give up."

Thinking back to the comments that the Grand Master and my roommate had made, warning me to be careful and even doubting my ability to handle myself, I found my mind made up. "I want them all. Every book you have available. I'll check them out today."

"Really? Just like that? You know, you have time to consider what you want to do for your Mastery yet. You don't have to jump right into it." The Lorekeeper looked from the book to me, and I could hear that same tone in his voice that I had with Tristifer and the Grand Master. The doubt, the disbelief. Sure, this time it might have been because of how quickly I had made up my mind, but something about it made me snap.

"Yes. I'm sure. I'll check them out today." Seeing my serious expression, the man could only nod. Handing him the book, I felt a shiver run down my spine and looked up. Freezing at the sight of gold. Once again, the piercing stare of Drakari gazed down at me from one of the many painted windows. This one depicted the wolf-God facing down the Demon God Kirogin, snarling in anger at the red and black figure. A shiver ran down my spine at the sight, and I turned away to follow the Lorekeeper.

Hours later I find myself sitting in one of the many study rooms located on the lower levels of the library, pouring over one of seven Conjuration books currently available in the Master's section. Apparently, two others were currently checked out to senior students, giving me a total of nine texts I could study. A number that was far, far lower than I had expected given the size of the library's inventory. *Even the Lorekeeper had been surprised by the low number of texts!*

There was a basic primer on the subject available in the lower levels of the library, but I had quickly dismissed it. Likely, all the information found within it would be covered in the more advanced texts I currently had in my possession. Either way, the lack of materials was both frustrating, and exciting. *A whole new realm of magic! Near completely unexplored!!*

The Lorekeeper had not been lying when he'd said it was a particularly complex subject, either. In first opening paragraph of the first text that I had been given, *On Creation, a Treatise of Conjuration* by Marek Sadon, it was openly stated that the school of magic was not for those afraid of research. The author, Master Sadon, asserts that Conjuration is not the act of creating, something from nothing, as many assume, but is based largely on the same principles as Alchemy.

In order to fully grasp the art of Conjuration, one much have a fundamental understanding of the natural world and the various materials and components found within it. The same is true for Alchemy. Using that knowledge, one can then change those materials using magic into something else entirely by combating the material's inherent "Will" to keep its shape. Master Sadon uses the example of a steel blade in his text, explaining how Master Mages would seemingly conjure such items from thin air.

The Mage would first change the air into the necessary components required to forge a blade of steel. That being iron, coal, and fire of sufficient heat to remove the iron's impurities. Then, you would need to create a hilt using wood and leather, or whatever you desire, really. While these items would not be conjured visibly, knowing about their role when creating a blade was important. Of course, the air would fight against your attempts to change its shape, making a Conjuration a school of magic that requires an exceptionally powerful Will. In theory, you could create any material or object with Conjuration, but eventually it would disappear when the magic fueling the spell faded.

"I asked for a challenge and got a near impossible task in return..." Flipping another page in the text, I rubbed my eyes. "I can see why so few Mages dedicated themselves to Mastering this particular school..."

It would take the average student countless hours of study before they even consider performing their first Conjuration. And that I doubted that it would be a particularly difficult one, either. To do such complicated magic during a crisis or a battlefield? Even the most exceptional of Masters would fail. You'd need to be a genius to Conjure anything with any real speed.

"Well, let it not be said that Richard Foxx is afraid of hardship..." Picking up the text, making sure to mark my page, I packed away the remaining six books into my satchel and made my way out of the small study room. The library was considerably less packed at this hour as it was now well passed the evening meal. Something my stomach was making me acutely aware of now that I noticed. *I must have been too focused on my studies...*

Waving to one of the few remaining Lorekeepers as I made my way towards one of the entrances of the library, opposite the way I had entered earlier, I stepped out into the now barren courtyard. Squinting as my eyes adjusted to the street's magic torch light, a far cry from the well-lit interior of the library, I debated on attempting to grab a last second meal at the dining hall.

*No, I'd likely arrive too late and miss my chance…*Figuring that I would have to go without tonight, but making a note to break my fast early tomorrow morning, I made my way back to the dormitories. Despite the barren nature of the courtyard, I made sure to walk with caution. You never know when a prank might be pulled, after all.

Thankfully, the trip back to the dormitory was quiet, likely a result of the late hours and poor morale of the first-year students, and I entered the building with little issue. Given my hungry state, I decided to forgo the stairs as I didn't want to work up too much of an appetite and chose instead to wait for the lift to arrive. "A poor excuse and you know it, Richard. Don't be lazy."

Deciding that it was too late to take the stairs as the lift was already on its way, I perked up when I heard the "ding" that alerted me to the arrival of the lift. However, I was forced to stepped aside to allow several of my peers to depart. Noticing a familiar blond in the midst, I nodded a greeting to Tristifer and made to step onto the magical disk, only to be stopped by a hand grabbing my shoulder

"*Yes*, Tristifer? Don't tell me we're locked out again…" Sighing in annoyance, I turned to meet my roommate's joyful gaze. Making sure to place my foot on the lift to keep it from departing without me.

"What? Oh! No, no. We're good there – I even got the Dorm Matron to repair the handle like you said. No, I was wondering if you'd eaten yet?" The question had me raising my brows in surprise, and my stomach rumbled silently. "We're going off campus for drinks, and food, so if you'd like to come…"

My head was already shaking the moment he started talking about leaving the campus, causing the blond to trail off. Ignoring his look of disappointment, I made my way on to the lift, giving a dismissive wave over my shoulder. "You know I don't do those sorts of gatherings. Thanks, though."

As the lift began to rise, I could hear the voices of Tristifer's companions, distant and muffled, and I scowled. "I don't know why you ask him, Tris. He never says yes."

"I know. But there's always hope he might someday." My roommate's optimistic response was the last of the conversation I could hear as I passed the threshold between floors. Part of me was surprised, even touched by his thoughts, and I considered what would happen if I *did* agree to one of his little outings.

The larger part of me crushed that down with the pointed reminder that I couldn't afford to leave the campus and eat or drink at one of the lavish inns and restaurants that surrounded it. That and I had seven new texts to read and take notes on, something far more important than a single night filled with alcohol and debauchery. Nodding in confirmation towards my own thoughts, and feeling a flash of embarrassment, as well as relief that I was alone, I stepped off the lift and made my way to mine and Tristifer's dorm room. I was pleasantly surprised to see that true to the blond man's word, the handle *had* been replaced.

"It was his fault in the first place…" Muttering to myself as I inserted my key to the lock, a useless gesture in a school filled with those that practiced magic, in my opinion, I entered the room and shut the door behind me.

Dropping my book-stuffed satchel on my bed and making a mental note that Tristifer and I needed to clean at some point in the future, I made my way to the small desk at the far end of the room. I stopped short when I caught sight of a small metal tray, similar to the ones used by the dining hall, on my desk. Glancing around the room in confusion, I activated my Sight and cautiously approached the dining tray. I could see a what looked like a folded letter, leaning innocently against it.

"What has that idiot done now?" Seeing no signs of magic, I sighed and reached down to pluck the folded letter off the small metal tray. Opening it and skimming the words written.

Looks like you're out studying late again. I don't know if I'll see you by the time I leave tonight, but I had figured you would say no to my offer anyway, like so many other nights. That said, I took the liberty

of accruing a dish I remember you liking. It's placed under a heating charm – from one of the cooks, don't worry. Thanks for the assistance earlier today, and apologies for the inconvenience!
  - Tristifer

Placing the letter to the side for the moment, I lifted the metal color off the small tray and peered at the contents within. It was a simple dish, just pan-seared salmon, mashed potatoes, freshly baked bread, and a small bowl of pottage, but the sight brought a small smile to my face. True to Tristifer's word, it was still warm due to the charms placed on it.

Grabbing the provided utensils, a simple fork and knife, and placing a cloth in my lap to prevent any messes – though unlikely – I began to cut the fish into smaller chunks. Blowing on it gently as I raised it to my mouth, I paused for a moment and glanced back at the book-stuffed satchel behind me. My stomach rumbling drew my attention back to the delicious meal in front of me.

"I guess I can study later..." Digging into the food with gusto, I reached over to grab Tristifer's letter and shook my head in bemusement. "Idiot. It's not like I wouldn't have unlocked it anyway. I live here too."

CHAPTER 3

"In conclusion, while magical energy may be drawn from the world around you in times of great need, it should be avoided unless absolutely necessary. Magic is about balance, after all. Often, seeking energy from outside sources, rather than one's self, can have horrible consequences." Professor Daylin, the university's premier Alchemist as well as Grand Master Ulirk's harshest critic, finished her lecture on *Magics of the Natural World and Their Effects on Potions and Alchemic Processes* to excited chatter and the raising of hands.

The many questions that I would have to sit through had me groaning inwardly in frustration and I turned my attention to the clock on the far wall. Professor Daylin may be brilliant but, like so many other professors at the university, her lessons were held back by the quality of her students. There were some outliers, of course, as fourth year students were hardly incompetent. This was especially true for those that survived the rigorous scholarship exams that took place once a semester. However, in my opinion, those exams didn't do enough.

A mandatory examination that determines what year you should be in would be a great addition. It would at least encourage the students to give their all rather than squeeze by year after year with barely passing grades – especially those with wealthy backgrounds. *Of course, I'm not sure how that would impact the other schools...*

Having never spoken to any of the students attending either the religious or general education colleges offered by the university, I had no idea what courses they provided. I knew that graduates from the first school often ended up in positions of prominence in the Church of Drakari and that the second school taught mercantile subjects as well as various trade-based skills, but that was the limit of my knowledge. *Maybe I should visit our sister schools to learn more about them? It would at least be more interesting than this...*

"Oh! That's all the time we have left. Make sure to read pages 205 through 235 in your texts and have a three-page essay on the benefits, and dangers, of accessing the magics of the natural world by next class." Professor Daylin's voice broke me from my thoughts, and I looked up at the clock again. I was shocked to see that almost thirty minutes had passed during my musings.

"Finally..." I muttered as I made a quick note of the assigned work, not bothering to write the pages down. I had already read the assigned textbooks of all my classes three times, after all. "Though, maybe a quick glance couldn't hurt."

Taking my time packing away my journals, I watched the students file out of the room. Almost a week had passed since I began studying the complex of Conjuration and the difference between self-study and my normal courses had me frustrated. Whereas my day-to-day schoolwork was tedious and boring, full of theories that I had already memorized, my nightly study sessions were exposing me to a whole new world of knowledge and information. I'd already read Master Sadon's introductory text twice in the last week and had recently moved onto his secondary volume, *On Creation Vol II, Key Materials to a Successful Conjuration.*

An uncreative title, a common theme when it came to Masters of the magical arts, I had noticed, but nonetheless a book filled with useful information. Sadly, I would have to return to my dorm to pick up the book as I had, on numerous occasions, been reprimanded for reading it during my courses. Especially by the Combat Magics instructor. Professor Aleric said that he would have my access to the library revoked if he caught sight of, or heard of, me reading the text outside of my free time.

"Ridiculous..." Seeing that the last of the students had filed out, I shoved my journal into my bag and stood. Making my way out of the classroom, I gave Professor Daylin a nod as I passed her.

The middle-aged woman, I think remember hearing that her and Grand Master Ulirk had graduated the same year, returned the gesture. However, she otherwise treated me with a cold indifference. Returning to her notes after seeing that I was the last student to leave the room. The coldness would have surprised me, but it had been a common occurrence with the Alchemy professor in the last week. I suspect my arrangement with the Grand Master being the reason.

Petty rivalries carrying on for decades and impacting student-teacher relations. The Grand Master wonders why I don't bother with social interaction. Shaking my head as I walked down the hall, I turned and made my way down a smaller, poorly lit, passage that offered a quicker route to the outside. They were common in many of the buildings, especially the older ones. Many students didn't utilize them, though, due to how cramped they were.

Outside of poor relations with two of my professors, life had been much the same the last week or so with only a single major difference – my Mastery subject. If the Grand Master had thought that finding something new and incredibly difficult would soothe my frustration towards my day-to-day courses, he was wrong. If anything, I'd become far more restless in the last week, especially after Professor Aleric made his threat.

The only thing intellectually stimulating any more is *Conjuration! The rest of it is just...boring.* I'd even begun to practice my artistic abilities in place of note taking! Several of my journals had become the victims of my, poorly composed, drawings. Most taking the shapes of things that interested me such as runes, weapons, various types of ships, and cats. Especially the larger ones.

"If it continues like this, I might find myself abandoning magic and pursuing a career in the arts!" Shaking my head and sighing, I debated on bringing my complaints to the Grand Master. However, I quickly dismissed the idea as soon as it came. The man had directed me to find a Mastery subject to fill my time with, complaining that I didn't have *enough* time to do so would come off as childish. And petty. *I could always complain about Professor Aleric and his unfairness...*

A promising thought, but again, I dismissed it. Even if the Grand Master heeded my complaints and took action against his staff, I would end up having even *more* time wasted. While the process *might* be entertaining, it would cut into my Mastery studying, leaving me more frustrated in the end.

"A distraction and a waste." Making my way out into the courtyard, I paused and considered my location carefully. In the last week or so there had been an uptick in spell-related pranks and "accidents." A result of the first-year students recovering from the hammering that the scholarship exams had given their morale. As a result, their antics had spread to covering all corners of the school, no doubt their idea of how to celebrate surviving the semester.

"It could be a much-needed distraction..." I muttered, hand still on the door handle and my body halfway out of the building. "And a good way to put my studies into practice..."

I wasn't sure if I could conjure anything, not yet, but there was only so much I could learn from a book. Putting my learning to use would be the best way to see how far I had come as well as how far I had to go. *And I could vent some of that frustration...*

I couldn't believe that I was seriously considering it. Utilizing magic on others as a form of venting was not unfamiliar to me, I had pranked Tristifer on more than one occasion due to his tendency to cause me grief, but other members of my peers? Specifically, my juniors? *They would probably start it. It's their fault for picking a fight they can't win.*

"True..." Glancing about the courtyard, I couldn't see any duels currently in progress. That didn't surprise me, as Professor Aleric would be wrapping up his most recent class soon. No one wanted to take the risk of being caught by the man. That said, I could see several students, male and female, eyeing me with interest.

What the hells, why not? Stepping out from the doorway, I made my way into the courtyard and stopped right at the center. An open challenge to anyone in the area. Several of the students seemed to bristle at the sight and I gave a half grin in response, sliding a hand through my hair to further taunt them. I knew what I was doing would be seen as provoking, and thus I lost the ability to claim they started it, but I found that I didn't care. Some part of me, a part I didn't know existed, was delighted at their anger and frustration.

Before I could open my mouth to issue a taunt of some sort, as I had grown bored of waiting, I found myself activating The Sight on reflex. Tugging apart a hastily thrown spell and backpedaling. I didn't have time to ponder its effects before I found myself unraveling yet another, and another, as three of the students attacked at once. Sending back my own hastily created spells, small things that would cause mild discomfort in their legs or arms, making it difficult to concentrate, I moved to position the three of them in front of me.

"Three on one? That's hardly fair!" Swatting yet another weave out of the air, this one much better constructed than the first three, I turned my attention to the one that had cast it and was surprised to find Selena. I hadn't recognized Tristifer's most recent fling when I had taken my brief survey of the area. "Is this because I undid your lock? Dismal work, by the way."

The casual dismissal of her skills had her gritting her teeth and glaring at me. Suddenly, I found myself, again, on the defense as a barrage of magic came flying towards me. The other three students, seeing that they fight had escalated between upper years, took a step back and decided to watch. Perhaps they were looking to learn something new? *Well, we can't disappoint our juniors, can we?*

Slashing through the barrage of spells with a, rather flashy, demonstration of my own power, I hurled two of my own at her. Quickly created minor hexes, overpowered to appear something far more sinister, causing her to panic and giving me a distraction to use to my advantage. Focusing my attention on the ground to her sides, I used my new knowledge of materials and their properties to alter the stone path. Changing the materials inherent shape to be similar to that of a mud pit – a deep one at that.

Dodging out of the way of my spells, not realizing that they were just overpowered versions of itching hexes, Selena ended up falling right into my quickly placed trap. Falling into the waist-high mud with a screech and a flail, cursing and screaming in confusion. I could tell that the three first years, and they had to be with their skills, were confused as well. Two of them had been standing right where she fell not moment's ago, after all.

"I do believe that that's my win." Calmly walking towards the screaming girl, I smiled down at her. Daring her to try and cast another spell.

My approach as well as my comment brought her screaming to a halt and she stared at me in confusion for a moment. Looking down at the mud, I saw her piece it together quickly. "Wait, you did this? How?!"

Nodding at Selena's question, I shrugged in response and glanced down to the mud pit. Not knowing what would happen should I dispel the magics changing the stone's properties while a human was in the mud, I cautiously reached out my hand to pull the girl out. Using a simple household charm to banish the mud off her before she had a chance to complain. She muttered a thanks as she looked herself over, not trusting me. I didn't blame her.

"Just some extra studying I've been doing." I explained, gesturing her away from the pits. I saw her attention switch from me and to the mud in question, her Sight activated as she examined it. Giving her a moment to see the weave, I allowed the magics holding the mud's shape to collapse. "It's basically just Transfiguration."

"Hey! I was…ugh. Well, I've never seen it done like that." Selena started to protest the spells ending but gave up on it halfway. Ending her use of the Sight and turning to look at me. "Most of the teachers just change small objects, not the *environment* during a duel."

"Yes, well, you were distracted. It wasn't that hard to sneak it in there." I could see that she was about to protest my dismissal, and I supposed it was rather advanced, for a fourth year. However, we all stiffened when a thunderous voice rang out in the court-yard, interrupting her.

"What in the Gods names did you do to that street?!" Professor Aleric roared, stomping down the stairs that led to the Combat Magics ward. He pointed angrily behind us as he did so, and I turned with dread to see large chunks of the stone pathway missing. No doubt because of pieces I had banished off Selena.

As one, the four other students, and others found around the courtyard, pointed to me. The bald professors' veins could be seen throbbing on the side of his head when he saw me, and I could tell that the already deep dislike he had for me had grown slightly deeper. *Just perfect...*

Thankfully, I wasn't punished too severely for damaging the pathway, as most of it had been due to be replaced anyway. Professor Aleric had been rather lenient, surprising me given how much he seemed to dislike me. Merely forced me to repair it with a spell that he'd taught the four of us on the spot, apparently one that he and his assistants used to fix the Combat Magics ward often. It wasn't as perfectly leveled as it had been before, which Professor Aleric made sure I knew, but it was repaired. However, learning the spell, getting it almost right, and dealing with the lashing that he'd given us, as well as grabbing a quick meal at the first venue available in the dining hall before they closed, took far longer than I had expected.

It wasn't until much later, long after the sun had set, that I found myself at the steps of the dormitories. Tired, both phys-ically and magically, all I wanted to do was collapse in my bed and sleep. That's why, when opening the mailbox assigned to me, I couldn't help the loud curse that escaped me at the sight of all too familiar handwriting. In all the excitement surrounding my Mastery, the scholarship exams, my brief stint at dueling, and studying, I had forgotten that the end of the semester had been approaching. As well as the month-long holiday that came after it.

"I'll have to schedule a meeting with my counselor soon..."

Muttering as I grabbed the envelope, the soft jingle of metal hitting metal lightly inside as I do, I stuffed it into my robe's inner pocket. Seeing no additional mail, I shut the mailbox and made my way up the lift to the third floor, the magical device arriving far quicker than normal due to the relatively dead hours of the night.

Opening the door to mine and Tristifer's room, I was surprised to see that the blond was still awake – and in our dorm room. Usually he would be out partying, celebrating the end of the semester with his many friends before the holiday. Instead he was sitting at his desk, quietly reading a book and taking notes, a lantern providing ample light for his side of the room. Upon hearing the door open and my first few steps into the room, the young man looked up and tilted his head in confusion at the sight of me frozen in the doorway.

"Richard? You alright?" Looking me up and down, he took in my somewhat haphazard appearance. "What happened to you?"

"Nothing, just practicing spells." Not exactly the truth, but not a lie. Thankfully, he seemed to accept that answer and nodded, though I saw caught sight of his green eyes narrowing at me for just the briefest of moments. So fast that it almost seemed like a fluke. I was reminded in that moment that, regardless of my comments, Tristifer was not as foolish as he appeared. He had no issues passing his classes, even if he didn't need to worry about the scholarship exam.

"Alright. Just be more careful, ok?" Turning back to his book, he ended the conversation there.

Shaking off the odd interaction, I made my way over to my desk and sat down, placing my satchel down beside me. Reaching into my robe to withdraw the envelope, I opened the wax seal and withdrew the single document that I knew it contained as well as pocketing the small pouch of coins. Tossing the envelope to the side and pocketing the pouch, I took a moment to prepare myself before unfolding the parchment paper reading the letter.

Richard. I'm happy to hear that you're doing well with your studies.

Unfortunately, I regret to inform you that you are not permitted to return home this winter solstice – your father was most clear on the matter. He, again, wishes for me to relay instructions – as well as his thoughts – towards your educational pursuits, but I have, as always, omitted those from this letter. Enclosed is a small sum that I hope helps you find lodgings for the holidays.

I'm sorry, lad.

- Rowan, Loyal Servant of the Foxx Family

Sighing and tossing the letter to the side near the envelope, I took a moment to compose myself and think. I would have to approach my counselor about the situation and see if I could, like last year, stay in the dormitory for the entirety of the winter solstice holidays. I knew that several professors did the same, taking the time to prepare for the following semester or partake in their own research projects. *At least I'll be able to do the same this year...*

Last year had been a miserable one. I had nothing to do after the second week of the holiday break, having finished all my course books by the end of the first week, and touched on any subjects I found lacking by the end of the second. The rest of break was spent exploring what limited library access I had, with most of the building shutdown due to renovations and the Lorekeeper's own personal projects, and trying to find a cheaper alternative to the inns and restaurants near campus. I had failed.

Yawning and feeling the exhaustion of the day hit me, I decided to tackle the issue tomorrow. Moving towards my bed and turning off the lantern that was positioned on desk, I removed clothes before climbing underneath the beddings and closing my eyes. As I drifted, to sleep, worn out by the day's events, I had the passing recollection that my counselor had been changed due to my Mastery study. *I'll have to visit the Grand Master tomorrow, then, to figure this whole thing out...*

As consciousness left me, I heard the slight creek of wood and the sounds of padded feet across the floor. A rustle of paper, a muttered curse, then darkness and a dreamless sleep. The sounds dismissed and pushed to the back of my mind as nothing more than

Tristifer getting ready for bed himself. *Idiot still needs to pack…*

CHAPTER 4

"Good afternoon, Mr. Foxx. Please, have a seat." The aging Mage gestured to the familiar dark red leather chair that sat across from his dark wood desk. I noted a small bit of damage to its frame, right near where one would usually rest their right hand, as I sat.

"Good afternoon, Sir. Was this chair damaged recently?" The question caught him off guard, but he recovered quickly and laughed lightly.

"Yes, but not beyond repair. A disagreement between myself and a colleague, is all. Now, you requested to see me?" Blinking at the shift in topic, I made a note to avoid Professors Aleric and or Daylin during the break, as they had both stayed last year, and nodded.

"Yes, Sir. It has come to my attention that my typical counselor has changed due to our arrangement. I believe that you now fill that role?" Seeing him nod, I continued with my request. "I'd like to stay here during break, Sir."

"Oh? You did that last year as well, correct?" I didn't ask how he had known that detail, assuming that it was on file somewhere and that he had looked into me after becoming my counselor, and simply nodded. "Well, there is a small fee required to do so, as you know. To pay for the unplanned cleaning and upkeep, but outside of this, you're more than welcome to stay for yet another holiday."

"Thank you, Sir." Reaching into my robe's inner pocket and removing the small coin pouch that had been included with my envelope, I offered the older Mage two silver coins. The snarling head of Drakari catching my eye in the light, but I shrugged it off and placed the coins on the desk. "This should cover it, if I recall."

"Yes, that'll more than do. Now, while I have you here, I figure that I should also inquire on how your extra studies have been going?" Leaning forward at his desk, the man placed his chin on his hands and looked at me curiously. "Have you chosen a topic? Professor Aleric had a most curious discussion with me this morning – Transfiguration, I assume?"

"It was a bit of that, yes Sir. But that's not the subject that I've decided to pursue – I've chosen Conjuration." I saw the Grand Master's eyes widen for a moment, but he quickly masked his shock. Shock and…something else. As quickly as it came, however, it was gone.

"A most difficult art – complex, demanding, and very dangerous." Tilting my head at his words, I furrowed my brow in confusion.

"Dangerous, Sir? Many of the Masters I've read say that Conjuration is no more dangerous than any other branches of magic unless, of course, you drain yourself too rapidly and deeply. But that can happen in any discipline." My words had the man nodding, and he looked bemused at me.

"True enough, Mr. Foxx, true enough." Conceding the point, the Grand Master looked in consideration around the room, as if he was contemplating where next to take this topic. But I caught the look in his eye again, the look that he knew something that he wasn't telling me. That there was some other point he wanted to make but didn't for some unknown reason.

"Sir? I hear the Master's Exam is coming up in a few months." Deciding that I couldn't outright ask him what he didn't want to tell me and making a note to read more about the dangers of Conjuration over break, I switched topics. "Near the end of the upcoming semester."

"Ah, yes. They are. Something that the professors and I are looking forward to." Seeing my look of determination, the older Mage sighed. "Mr. Foxx, you're not nearly ready to participate."

"Sir – please. I wish to take part. It's months away, I'll surely be ready by then!" I protested, the memory of Rowan's letter flashing in my mind. "Give me a chance to prove what I can do, please!"

There must have been something in the way that I had said that that caught the older man's attention, because the Grand Master paused in what he was going to say and considered me carefully. His grey eyes searching my brown closely – intensely. For a moment, those grey eyes seemed to flash yellow and I had the same feeling that I did in the library and dorms – like I was being laid bare. Finally, the man began to speak again. Gentle, yet just as unwavering.

"Mr. Foxx – Richard – you've done much to prove yourself in your time at our university, more than any other student that I've seen in my years as Grand Master, but this? This is beyond you." Seeing me about to protest, the greying Mage lifted his hand and gave me a hard stare. "No. That is my final answer."

"I understand, Sir." My disappointment and frustration were not hidden, nor did I try to make them so. I could only stare at the dark wooden surface of the Grand Master's desk, feeling the man's eyes bore into me.

"Good. In time you will be able to take the exam, Mr. Foxx. But this is not that time. Explore your chosen subject, expand your knowledge of its secrets. Then, deliver the greatest performance this school has ever seen." I know his words were meant to be encouraging, and I did feel my spirits lift slightly at them, but it all came crashing down the moment Rowan's letter again flashed in my mind.

I want to prove myself. I want to prove what I can do. To whom, I don't know. Is it myself, my father, this school, my peers? I just don't know. I wanted the chance, is all. The chance to show the world that I was destined to do more, to be better. To be the best. But it felt like I was being held back repeatedly from doing so.

"I will, Sir. I'll show the school, and the world, what I can do when the time comes." I lifted my gaze up and to his forehead, giving the illusion that I was looking into his eyes. I didn't want to have that feeling again. To have that soul-piercing stare see right through me.

"Excellent. I look forward to that day. In the meantime, however, I ask you to be careful. Can you promise me that? Keep your limitations in mind." The words made me pause, and I risked a glance into his eyes, and quickly looked aback upwards to his forehead at the sheer intensity that I found in them. The knowledge of something unspoken was there. A secret that had been danced around since the beginning of this conversation.

What is the danger of Conjuration, Sir? What aren't you telling me? I questioned, but no words were spoken. Instead, I found myself nodding my head to his words and looking at the desk yet again. "May I be excused, Sir?"

"Yes, Mr. Foxx. Have a good rest of your day." As I stood from the dark red-leather chair and made my way to the door, I could feel his gaze burning into my back. It took all the willpower I had to keep my pace measured and calm, to avoid panicking at the intensity of his stare. I quickly bowed my head in respect and made my exit.

I rushed back to the dormitories as soon as I closed the door, uncaring of how it looked or what people thought of me. All I knew is that I had to get away from those eyes. Those eyes that saw so much and held so many secrets. Still, as I fled, the question repeated in my mind once more. *What is the danger of Conjuration, Sir?*

"Hey, Richard? What are your plans for the break?" The sudden question from my roommate nearly had me dropping the book I was reading. It was a collection of poems written by various authors over the centuries, something I had grabbed to take my mind off magic. Shrugging at the blond-haired man, who had just finished packing for his own holiday and was merely waiting for his escort, I continued where I had left off. The lack of verbal response must have frustrated him because I heard Tristifer sigh and make his way over. Tapping on the corner of my desk to get my attention and tearing me, yet again, away from my distraction.

"Oh, come on, you're not staying on campus again are you?" Sighing in frustration at the question, and seeing that the man wouldn't leave me alone, I quickly noted the page number and closed the book to give him my undivided attention.

"Yes, just like I did the year prior. Why?" I saw his green eyes narrow and he placed his hand on his chin. A pose I associated with the blond when he was plotting something. "No. Whatever it is you're thinking, stop. The answer is no."

"Come on, Richard! You don't even know what I was going to suggest." Raising his hands in frustration, the other man moved over to his bed, now lacking any sort of coverings, and sat down. Staring at me for a long, hard moment, he suddenly nodded, and a determined look crossed his face. "Stay with my family for the break. My father won't mind, hells, you might find it enjoyable, even. We have a very sizeable library."

The proposal caught me off guard and I found myself staring at the blond with some shock. A bright smile had crossed his face, though a small flush had covered his freckled cheeks, likely from embarrassment or nervousness. He appeared genuine, as he always did when asking me to do things, and for a moment I considered saying yes.

"No, no that's ok. I'll stay on campus. I have a personal project that I'm working on and want to see it finished before term begins again." I found myself saying after a moment's consideration, and my words caused Tristifer to frown. "Thank you, though. It was… kind of you, Tristifer."

"Are you sure, Richard? I just…Don't want you to be alone all winter solstice, again." He spoke slowly, keeping his eyes on me and watching my reactions. "I never see you go home is all – it worries me."

The concern shouldn't surprise me. It wasn't the first time I've experienced it from Tristifer, though it was the first time he was so obvious about it. However, part of me couldn't help but feel it was suspiciously timed. My brain went into overdrive as I studied his face, staring into his green eyes with my own dark brown, causing the flush on his cheeks to darken. Eventually, he looked away and I had puzzled together why he broached the subject so suddenly.

"You read the letter – didn't you?" At his hesitant, regretful, nod, I sighed and cursed my lack of foresight. "I should have hidden the damned thing. Is that the only reason, then? You felt bad, maybe pity, for me?"

The accusation seemed to anger him, an emotion that I've never seen on Tristifer's face, now that I think of it, and he scowled at me. Narrowing his green eyes and shaking his head furiously as he clenched his fist, he bit his lip and looked like he was going to say something but held back. Closing his eyes and taking a deep breath to calm himself instead. After a few moments, he opened his eyes again, appearing considerably calmer and less furious.

"No. Look – I'm sorry for reading the letter, ok? It's just…I don't really know anything about you, and we've lived together for *two years*, Richard! I know you're smart, you're always studying, and you, for some reason, dislike me, but that's it. I get it, you know. I can be a handful sometimes. A little too eager to let loose, perhaps trouble prone, and I'm sorry. I just…. Wanted to be your friend, I guess."

He took another long moment to compose himself after his small rant, taking several deep breathes to calm himself down. While he did so, I looked back at all the conversations I'd had with Tristifer over the last two years and tried to see them in a different light. Whereas before I'd saw him as an idiot that stumbled his way through life, getting by with help from both his parent's money and his own, wasted, talents, I now saw him as a *well-meaning* idiot. The rest mostly still applied, and we'd really have to address his wasted potential before graduation, but the well-meaning part really did make a difference.

"I'm sorry, Tristifer. I've been unfair to you. Unfair, and an ass." I said, and the admission caught him off-guard, nearly having him fall from his bed in shock. "I still won't be coming to your home this break, though. Plans have already been made and all. But, this summer, maybe? If you'll have me, that is."

"Absolutely! Do you think you could handle me for three *more* months, Richard?" The smile he sent me was bright as the sun, and

I found it somewhat contagious.

"Well, almost an entire year with you will be quite the challenge. I'll do my best to try and not banish you into The Void." A small smile on my face was more than enough to convince him that I was, *mostly,* joking. Suddenly, for the first time since my arrival at the university two years ago, my roommate and I had an actual conversation.

It was almost therapeutic, in a way. Talking to someone about something outside of the day-to-day ongoings of the university and all that came with it. We quickly established ground rules, no talking about classes or the professors, outside routine gossip, for instance. As we talked, I learned that Tristifer was quite the writer. Well, in his own words. In exchange I told him about my own developing skills as an artist, which he was surprised to learn. *Let it not be said that those long, boring hours in lectures don't go unused.*

When the time came that he had to go, I admit only to myself that I was sad and disappointed. I cursed the wasted months and years really that I had unfairly judged and disregarded the man. I considered that, maybe, I had done the same to many of the people at the university. *Starting next semester, I'll try to be better.*

That said, the conversation with Tristifer had proved a welcome, if unexpected, distraction from the worries that plagued me. The meeting with the Grand Master was still fresh in my mind, as were the feelings that I had both expressed, and experienced, during it. I wanted to prove myself to all those that doubted me and my place at the university. Notably, I wanted to prove myself to my father, who never supported my decision to attend in the first place.

How? How can I prove myself? How can Conjuration help me do it? I needed to do something that no student had ever done, something only a Master could claim to have accomplished. It would need to be a demonstration of my abilities, my creativity, and both my power and my skill.

"What I need is something extraordinary." Turning my gaze to the painted-glass window that separated my dorm room from the outside world, my attention was drawn to the sight of a small moth fluttering around the glass. Drawn to the light from my lantern but unable to reach it. My mind began to swim with the possibilities.

How hard would it be to conjure something small like that? Like a moth, or maybe a small bird? Surely not much more difficult than a complex piece of jewelry or intricate set of clothing, something Masters of Conjuration had done in previous years. All you needed to know was what the animal, or insect in this case, was composed of. And that wasn't too far-fetched to find in a library as massive as the one on campus. *Surely someone has done a study on the organic make up of life in the 1,300 years this institute has been running...*

A new idea would mean more research, of course, and more time dedicated to the study of not just Conjuration, but the natural world. Creating a moth from the very air, converting the invisible substance to the materials required to form life, even small life, was surely something that even the highest level of Mages would be impressed by. The Grand Master would be awestruck at such a feat, I'm sure. *As would my father.*

"It's not as if the idea isn't sound, either. There's plenty of records and documents that support the idea that organic life is made up of common elements." It could work, and it would be extraordinary. None of the books had anything similar, as far as I know. *I'll have to check.*

Glancing out the window yet again, I watched the moth flutter about in the air for several moments, considering what it might take to create something similar. A sudden urge to yawn struck me, and I glanced at the clock on the wall of our dorm room. Seeing the lateness of the hour and feeling a sense of amazement that I had talked to Tristifer for so long, I decided to start my studies first thing in the morning. Making myself ready for bed, and extinguishing the lantern on my desk, I took a moment to admire the campus at night through the window, imaging what the future might hold.

I'll show you what I can do. Laying down in my bed and pulling the soft coverings up to my chin, I wondered absent-mindedly who the "you" was in this situation. The thought lingered with me until sleep claimed me, leading me to blissful dreams of success and acknowledgement from shadowy figures.

CHAPTER 5

After waking and recollecting my thoughts, I revisited the crazy idea of conjuring life itself. It would require a large amount of research as well as preparation, something I had more than enough time to do, given the holidays. A small part of me whispered that what I was considering was, likely, blasphemy of the highest levels. The creation of life was the realm of the Gods, if you believe the Church. But the larger part of me dismissed that whisper as nonsense.

"If it's created by magic, is it truly alive? Is it real? Does a cup, truly, become a cat even if a Master of Transfiguration changes its shape?" Muttering to myself as I rose from my bed, I grabbed my supplies and made my way to the dorm bathroom to take care of my morning business.

Once that was done, and I had dressed in my standard grey robes and black boots, I grabbed my satchel and made my way out of the dormitories. The campus was, for the most part, barren of any students outside the handful of individuals that had yet to leave, would be staying as research assistances, or, like me, didn't have much choice. *At least I can take the fast route to the library then, I doubt my display at the courtyard has the first years apprehensive about initiating a duel.*

After a moment's consideration, I decided that perhaps taking the longer route was prudent. It was better to avoid risk, after all. Looking around the campus, taking in the sight of its tall spires and immaculately cleaned buildings, magic made keeping white stone spot-free triflingly easy, I couldn't help but appreciate Libira's climate. Unlike the northern city-states, the Holy

City experienced a very mild winter solstice. Snow was rare, and never lasted long before melting away. Freezing temperatures had occurred maybe twice in the last century, making it the ideal location for year-round learning.

Rounding one of the many smaller buildings that made up the university's, admittedly lacking, shopping area, I entered what students called the "Old Campus." The name, while unoriginal, wasn't too far from the truth. It was the district in which the library was located, arguably the oldest building on campus, and many of the buildings around were also quite ancient. *The dormitory might rival them, however. I think it was the original Church living quarters.*

As such, many of the buildings here had the same architectural style as the library and the dormitory. They had, at one point, served a religious purpose, though I never cared to learn the details. Painted glass windows, many of which had had their depictions changed to reflect their field of study rather than their original religious ones, and tall spires with hard lines and white stone were common. The renovation costs to change their usage had to have been staggering, and likely were according to the tuition price, though I suspect magic had been used.

"Speaking of which..." Sighing to myself as I walked, I finally turned my thoughts to the subject that I had been avoiding - using magic to conjure life.

While the theory was sound, though I would need a wide range of books, the idea itself was...somehow disturbing to me. Something about it, about conjuring even a moth, gave me pause and caused the hair on my arms to rise. *And then there is the issue of the moth itself...*

"Too damn common. A moth is too common in Libira." I couldn't use the small insect to showcase my abilities, even if I conjured it right in front of a crowd. It would be too easy to accuse me of staging it, of summoning it from my dorm room and into my hand or some other trick. I needed something uncommon, something that there would be no way for me, either with my limited finances or with magic, to obtain. "Another thing to research, then..."

Glimpsing the tall spires of the library over the tops of the other buildings in the district, I felt my apprehension grow. Could I do this? *Should* I do this? I didn't even know where to begin the process of conjuring a *moth,* let alone something more exotic! What if I messed up and the spell lashed back at me? The thoughts almost had me turning around and fleeing to back to the dorm, putting the whole thing behind me. *It's not too late to pick up Enchantment instead...*

"No. No I can do this. I just need to research it carefully, maybe learn stabilizing runes and rituals to assist me." I nodded at one of the assistants that passed me by as I finally entered the courtyard that led to the library. The young woman gave me a curious look, likely wondering why I was still on campus, but returned my nod and dismissed me a moment later.

Quickly making my way up the steps of the library and towards the doors, I considered what I might need to research and where I might find it. Pushing open the doors and entering the library, I paused mid-step, finding that I had started towards the Master's section without even realizing it. *Would I need to go up there for what I'm looking for? Surely even the lower levels have the information I need.*

Deciding to approach the center ring and ask the Lorekeepers for assistance rather than risk pointlessly searching for the information, I looked for a free one. Seeing one of the library's caretakers just filing paperwork, made my way over and cleared my throat to get their attention. The man looking up at me with silent annoyance at the interruption but putting the papers on a nearby desk and nodding to me.

"Ah, excuse me? Could you maybe tell me where I could find books on the composition of animals? An autopsy, material study, or something similar?" The question had the man looking at me in confusion, and I knew that it was an odd request, but tapped his chin and looked around us.

"Certainly, Sir. But what sort of animals are you looking for? Genus and climate." I had to stop and think at that. I hadn't really considered what I would conjure instead of the moth, only that it needed to be rare and hard to obtain.

"Something exotic – savanna or rainforest, maybe? As for genus..." Well, I always did like cats. The larger ones particularly. "Feline, preferably. Larger breeds."

Nodding his head at me as I explained what I was searching for, the red-robed Mage gestured for me to follow him to the other staircase of the library – the one that led to the non-Master sections. Following the man and feeling relief that I had asked and not pointlessly looked for the information where it likely would not have been. Our journey had us traveling up two flights of stairs and down several rows before coming to a stop in front of a small section of texts and scrolls.

"Here's what you're looking for – is there anything else I might be able to assist you with?" The Lorekeeper said, obviously curious as to why I, a student over winter solstice, was searching this information. It really was an odd request.

"No, thank you. This should be all that I need." I said, and the red-robed man nodded at me and began to walk away – pausing just before he'd left the row.

"You are aware that you may not check out any of the texts during the break, correct?" Seeing my nod at his question, he continued. "Good. If you need anything else, please be sure to contact myself or the other Lorekeepers. Leave the book where you found it if able and have a good day."

With that, the man continued his walk, heading back the way we came and down to the first floor to continue his work. A large part of me was curious as to what the Lorekeepers did during the day, when they weren't stocking the shelves and checking over the condition of returned texts, but I was more amazed at their ability to recall and or locate specific resources. *It has to be more than just the spell I saw weeks ago. How else could he have found these?*

Shaking my head to clear myself of the random thoughts and turning my attention to the shelves before me, I slid my finger across their spines, reading their titles silently to myself. After the third text I found one that looked promising and removed it from its location, making sure to pull the book beside it out to mark my space, and skimmed through it. After several dozen pages I found an entry that looked promising. It discussed the anatomy of a leopard, with detailed illustrations to show what the text described.

"Disgusting..." Seeing the organs of another living thing was not something I ever wanted to do, even if hand drawn. I wasn't a hunter, or fisher, by any means. As such I had never really considered what my insides or the insides of another creature looked like. "But...helpful, I suppose."

Knowing what I was supposed to be creating, in detail, would help me with the actual construction of it during the Conjuration process. That said, the inability to take this book or any other with me posed a small problem. *I need to study it thoroughly to get it right. Unless there is some sort of charm or spell that I can use to create copies of words and drawings...*

"Not a bad idea." Grabbing the text – making sure I left my marker yet – I made my way downstairs and towards the small ring at the center of the library. *Hopefully the Lorekeepers have a spell like that.*

It turns out that the library's keepers *did* have a spell like that, and that would explain how all the texts looked pristine despite their supposed age. I was able to get several pages of my chosen book copied without issue, including the drawings, and I also made sure to grab some resources on material composition. Sadly, only a *human* one was available. That meant I would have to do mathematics to find the right amounts for a leopard.

"More research and more calculations..." Sighing, I looked over the drawings that I had obtained. They covered all angles of leopard, allowing me to visualize the feline while conjuring it. That would make the process far, far easier. "Now if only I didn't have to worry about the organs."

Entering spreading out the copies of the drawings on my desk, I debated on pestering the Lorekeepers again for more detailed drawings of animal organs. Specifically of a feline's. However,

I quickly dismissed that idea and looked through the various drawings that I already had. They should suffice, being quite detailed and, like the exterior drawings, covering all angles. I was just overly cautious. Still, with proper visualization, careful mathematics, and maybe a stop by the medical ward to see if they had feline organs to examine, this all appeared possible. *In theory. Possible in theory.*

And that was a phrase I was beginning to feel more and more anxious about. Everything I was doing was just that, *theory.* I could obtain the necessary control and power needed using runes and wards, in theory. And I had a fundamental enough understanding of magic and spell weaves to pull this off, in theory. And I could *conjure life from the very air utilizing basic principles,* in **theory**.

"Am I really going to do this?" I asked myself, staring out the windows of my dorm room. My eyes were drawn to the moths fluttering just outside the stained glass. "It would be so much simpler to just conjure the moth and be done with it."

Simpler to fake, too. No one would believe you – they'd laugh in your face. Scowling, I looked to the pages on my desk. Spreading them apart further to allow myself to see all of the parts and pieces I needed.

"No. No one will laugh or doubt me after this." I knew that for certain. Not even my father could question my decision to attend a magical university if – *when* – I pulled this off. "He'd have to be amazed. Amazed and proud. And the Grand Master? Surely, he'd let me skip ahead, maybe even just forgo the classes all together."

Wouldn't that be the dream? I could be like the assistants and professors here, working on my own research, exploring uncharted territory. Never touching another basic treatise on magic again. *Professor Foxx – I like the sound of that. Maybe even Master Foxx.*

Emboldened by the idea, I took a seat at my desk and got to work. "First, I need to stabilize the field and draw power from the air around me – I won't have enough to do this on my own. Then I need to…"

Muttering away as I wrote and crafted the various runes for my wards, drawing from my extracurricular studies as well as the course material I had read ages ago. Slowly, I began to see theory turn into reality. It really was just the basics, after all. *I can't believe I was intimidated by this…*

Still, there was a great deal of work to be done before I could truly begin. Even with a stabilizing rune, a clear visualization of the animal, both internal and external, as well as drawing on the power of the world around me, I had to account for unexpected variables. What if someone knocked on the door mid-way through the spell? What if my weave was off by even the slightest variable? What were my safety circles? I needed to create an advanced warding system – one that would protect the room and myself from anything going wrong.

"Didn't Professor Daylin talk about this in her lecture? I swear I had summary of the important parts…" Digging in my journals for the text in question I cursed my lack of attention in the last week of classes. Still, I knew that I had at least written the ward circle down. "Ah! Here it is. The wards are used for Alchemy experiments, but they should suffice here. An exploding potion and spell are essentially the same when it comes down to it."

Having gathered all the necessary materials, or at least most of them, I got to work crafting my ward circles as well as adding the various runes I would be utilizing during my spell. As I worked, part of me really wished that I had taken more time to study Enchantment and warding rather than only taking a glance at them. *I'll modify the circles tomorrow after stopping at the library again. I'm sure there's a text somewhere in there that would help me achieve the results I'm looking for.*

As I worked, I felt my earlier unease at the idea of conjuring life fade away and be replaced with confidence. If it was this easy, how could it be wrong? It was just Control, Will, Skill, Intent, and Power after all – like all magic. *I might even try it tomorrow, depending on how my time at the library goes.*

A shiver ran up my back at the thought and for a moment I felt the unease return as well as a sense of…something unusual. However, I dismissed both feelings a result of being tired and having skipped both breaking my fast and my evening meal. I hadn't been terribly hungry due to the organs I'd seen, drawings or not. *I'll just get some rest. I've done most of the work already and I'll just end up changing it all after the library anyway.*

Getting up from my desk and taking one more glance out the window, I ignored the moths entirely. Turning my gaze upward to look at the depiction in my dorm room's stained-glass window. This one depicted the twelve original beings who had created the world prior to Drakari's ascension, and for a moment I pondered if the Gods had just been advanced Mages from another world. Perhaps Mages that had done exactly what I'm planning to do now? The thought filled me with excitement as I dressed for bed and laid down, turning off my lantern.

As I fell into a dreamless sleep, my mind wandered, and I couldn't help but wonder what Tristifer was doing currently. Perhaps what I would have been doing had I had gone with him. *Probably lazing about. I doubt he would have that far ahead, the idiot...*

The next day, in the late afternoon, I had everything I needed for the Conjuration attempt. I thought long and hard about what I would need to pull it off, even if I should get a professor or the Grand Master to supervise me but thought against it. They would likely attempt to stop me or try to talk me out of it. Frankly, I think they would be overreacting if they did, too. *If it goes wrong, it goes wrong, and I have a mess to clean up. That's all there is too it. The conjured items, or animal, in this case, will disappear after some time anyway. I'll just rework and try again.*

"It's not like spells don't go wrong when you first attempt them, anyway." Nodding as I finished drawing the improved and modified ward circle I had created, I stepped back to admire it in full.

The trip to the library had been beneficial, as I suspected it might. A quick search in the Master's section early in the morning provided the needed runes and patterns to improve the safety and stability of my spell, as well as providing additional power to my weave if needed. Several of the runes had been a bit confusing but, after cross referencing them with other sources, I was confident that they would work.

"Let's just hope I don't conjure *half* a leopard. I would hate to have *that* be my first attempt…" Muttering as I moved to position the various illustrations I had obtained across from where I would be standing at the center of the ward circle. "Right, that should be everything. Remember to be confident, Richard. Confidence and Willpower."

Nodding to myself and taking a deep breath, I activated my Mage Sight to have a better view of what it was I was attempting to do. I could see the bright – almost blinding – glow of my circle's wards as I activated them, and a small dome took shape around me before spreading to the room itself. After the walls of the dorm room took on a small, dull, bluish hue, I knew the wards were in place.

"Alright, Richard. Here we go." Gathering my power and directing my Intent towards a small area I had cleared for just this purpose. Slowly I began to bend the air around me to my Will, forcing it to comply with my demands and take the shape I desired.

The effort, immediately, began to drain me. I could feel even my, admittedly large, pool of magic dropping fast – faster than I originally calculated for. I felt a moment of panic hit me, and the spell's weave faltered for a second, but I quickly corrected it and forced myself to calm down. *You prepared for this, Richard! Activate the other circle!*

Directing a small portion of my power to the ground beneath me, towards the secondary circle of my wards and the runes located there, I Willed them to activate. These were the ones I had created today, based on my trip to the library this morning, and just in case this exact problem arose. Almost immediately once the outer circle activated, the bright green in the corner of my vision letting me know, did I feel a change in the magic filling the air. My magic pools stopped falling immediately, even starting to replenish.

Good – its working! The secondary ward was a complicated one, something I had found in an old journal at the back of the runes section of the library. It was supposed to draw in power from the natural world and use it to fuel spells and even your own magical reserves if needed. Useful for spell weaves this complex – and also the subject of Professor Daylin's most recent lecture. *I just needed to refine the drawing I copied.*

Time passed and I kept my focus and Will sharp, my eyes trained on the location I had chosen for this creature to appear. Slowly, yet surely, I could feel…something taking shape as the air began to coalesce around where I desired, obeying my Will. The mental strain, something I had failed to consider, was great, but I tried to keep myself focused on my task.

A leopard. A leopard. I want a leopard. Imaging all the details I had gathered about the creature I wanted I kept my mantra going. Using it to try and keep my focus even as the minutes wore into what was becoming hours. I felt sweat drip down my face and back as the room heated up from the concentration of magic.

Slowly, my mantra became more and more difficult to maintain, as did my focus. I could feel the mental strain getting to me as standing in the same position for so long and casting the same weave wore at me. I pushed more power into it, more Will, as I tried to get the spell to *hurry up and finish!*

Whatever had begun to form at my desired location had halted, too. No doubt due to my wandering thoughts and impatience, and I forced myself to refocus and concentrate. *Come on, Richard! Just a little more!*

"I just need to finish the weave. That's all I need to do. It's nearly done! Just a little more and I can take a break." Muttering to myself, my focus slipped once again. This time I caught myself looking at the depiction in my stained-glass window.

Conjuring a leopard is difficult enough – how did you do it with a human? I questioned the twelve figures. They, of course, did not respond. A felt a sudden slipping sensation in my mind and panicked once again as the weave began to collapse. My lapse in focus breaking my connection with both the spell *and* the wards beneath me.

I felt the magic inside the room whirling as the wards suddenly gave out. The magics they were using pulling inwards, latching on to one another. The safety and stabilizing wards combined with the nature magic siphoning ward, using the near endless power they provided to keep themselves going. I tried to pull them apart, but to no avail. My lack of knowledge on runes and wards preventing me from being successful. To my horror, I felt the weave, still partially attached to me, anchor itself to both my magical core *and* the wards below me. I felt my panic grow at the sensation.

"Shit!" Scrambling, I grabbed a letter opener off Tristifer's desk, the closest one to me, and cut a long, thin, line across the ward circles. Ruining them and destroying their integrity.

My Sight, still activated, saw the wards fail, however the safety and stabilizing ones went first. I saw, too late, the power they were holding back erupt forth. There was a bright flash of light and immense pain as I felt the full weight of the magic inside the room suddenly be unleashed from what I now realized was the only thing keeping it contained. A thunderous roar exploded in my ears – along with the sounds of…something else.

Then, nothing.

CHAPTER 6

Pain. Pain and warmth. Not exactly the feelings that I associated with the afterlife, though I guess I couldn't really give my opinion on it. I hadn't expected to end up anywhere particularly pleasant, given my last actions on the planet had been a spit in the Gods' faces. Still, the stabbing pain throughout my body didn't bode well for whatever grim future awaited me. *Alright, Richard... Time to face judgement.*

Having a moment, I decided to take stock of the situation. A quick tensing of my body showed that I was, as far as I could tell, whole and potentially able to move – though my arms and legs refused to listen. The most I could do was breathe, currently, and what I could smell wasn't very reassuring.

I was not a tremendously violent man by any means. Sure, I had my bouts of anger, but never ones that drove me to commit violence. That said, I knew the smell of blood – metallic and rusty. Some educators believed that was a result of the substance touching skin and not the smell of the liquid itself... *Focus, Richard!*

Mentally smacking myself for getting side-tracked, I focused on the smell again. It was strong, strong and close. In fact, I would haphazardly guess that the warmth I was feeling around me was in fact the source of the smell, meaning that I was lying face first in what I assumed was a puddle of it. The only question was, who did it belong to?

Stupid question! My body seemed to scream at me as the stabbing pain returned. It didn't have a singular source, like a blade wound. It came from my entire being, from my toes to my ears, everything cried out in pain. I needed to open my eyes, I had to see my condition. I had to find out...

*The leopard...*The thought of the weave I had been crafting brought energy back to me. It had been nearly done, right? What had happened to the leopard? *Are they man-eating animals?*

With renewed strength, largely due to fear, I admit, I gritted my teeth and opened my eyes. Squinting through the sudden light, which blinded me for a moment, I was shocked to find myself not in some fire-filled underworld or gray void, but my dorm room. A room that looked quite different from how I last remembered it. *By all that is holy...*

It looked as though a storm had passed through but focused its power into this tiny location. The walls were in shambles, with entire sections of them broken clean through and allowing me to see into the rooms that lay beyond. Other sections, from what I could see without moving my neck too far, where littered with deep gashes. It was as if a large blade had been swung wildly and with great strength. What furniture I could see was damaged beyond the repair of most magics, being completely shattered, or destroyed by whatever force had been unleashed. The stained-glass window was destroyed, blown outwards I imagine by the explosion of power.

Did...Did I do this? I remembered cutting the warding that prevented the whole thing from collapsing, a stupid move on my part, I now realize, to prevent the nature magic wards from feeding the spell weave further. I had feared that it would cause a great explosion or mutate the spell. *Well, one of those was right. Looks like nothing was conjured at least. That's a relief. Explaining this, however...*

Wait...What's that? I could hear something else now, commotion from outside the building. It sounded like shouting, and maybe running? *Of course, you idiot. You damned near leveled half the floor – what did you expect?*

A glint in the corner of my eye caught my attention and, with great difficulty, I turned my head to look at what had once been my door. It was, like the walls and furniture, completely devastated, shattered into pieces. The frame was barely holding together, and the door itself was near destroyed. Only small pieces of it were held up by one of the three original hinges, the source of the glint that had caught my eye. I wasn't too surprised to find the destruction had spread that far. What I was surprised about, however, was what lead to the doorway.

Pawprints, or what I assumed were pawprints. They were made in the very blood that pooled around me, meaning that whatever had made them had to have been close to me. I couldn't see them very clearly, but could make out that they started out normal, like an animal of some size, and led up to the doorway itself. That's when things changed.

They turned around, leading back towards me in a second set, mutating and changing as they did so. They grew bigger, less feline. More something...else. Something I haven't seen before. Something with large, almost talon-like, claws from what I could tell. Some of the damage to the room, specifically the gashes, took on a new meaning.

Where I once saw destruction from a spell that had gone wrong or been overpowering, I now saw a beast that had gone mad. Large cuts in the wall became gashes from talons that were too long, too sharp, for any natural creature. The furniture became inconveniences, obstacles to be removed to allow a Beast to grow even larger. *That means...*

My gaze snapped back to the doorway and I felt a cold chill run down my spine at the remains of my door. A door that would have been just another obstacle, easily overcome by this now-towering construct of rage. *By the Gods, what have I done...?*

It was at this moment that I caught sight of the Grand Master running towards my room, his eyes wide and panicked at the sight of the demolished barrier. Following him was a small army of people, several of which I recognized as my teachers. The group only paused for a moment to gape at the destruction before moving in, the Grand Master leading with a small team of what I knew to be the school's on-site medical Mages. Experts in healing magics.

"Richard! Gods lad, what happened?!" the Grand Master said,

standing off to the side as the medical Mages examined me.

I could only stare up at him helplessly, words failing to be spoken. Both for a lack of ability, and a lack of effort. I didn't want to admit it. Not to him. Not to the man that had shown me trust, believed in me when I said I wouldn't overreach. That I would be careful. So, I said nothing, merely closed my eyes and let the blissful sensation of healing magic wash over me. I heard one of the medical Mages speaking, no doubt detailing my list of injuries to the Grand Master, but I was too tired and shaken to pay attention.

Instead, I let myself be lured off by the sweet temptation of sleep, encouraged by the healing magics that were engulfing me. Standard practice among medical Mages – send you into a coma so they don't have to deal with you. I was grateful for the escape from my inevitable interrogation.

Still, as I drifted off towards rest, all I could see were those pawprints changing. Enlarging, growing into something deadly, something monstrous. Something that now roamed freely across the school, unknown, unseen, and amongst a people that were entirely unprepared. I had to warn them! I couldn't rest just yet!

"W-wait…" I spoke, though it was more of a croak than words. My eyes opened and I looked to around to try and find the Grand Master, only to see him outside the door talking to one of his peers. I couldn't make them fully, but it appeared to be my Alchemy teacher – Professor Daylin. "Sir…"

"Hush, you need to rest." One of the healers told me, pushing me down as I attempted to rise with little success. He was strong, far stronger than I would have been on a good day I suspect. Still, I had to pass on a warning of some sort.

"Creature…" I raised an arm with all the energy I could muster, pointing at the floor behind the healer. At the pawprints, now scrapped and tarnished by booted feet, and their sudden change. I begged them to understand, to see.

"Rest, Richard. You'll be alright." The healer said. I could tell that my warning hadn't reached him, as he did not turn to look where I pointed. Instead, he placed his hand on my forehead and I felt my exhaustion grow – his magic overpowering me in my weakened state.

As I fell towards blissful unconsciousness, I kept my eyes locked on the Grand Master and my finger pointed towards the prints. I had to let him see, to warn him. Even as my own body began to shut down and fall into a deep sleep. It was only at the very end, when I could remain conscious no longer, that the man turned. I saw his gray eyes narrow and follow my finger to the prints before they widened. He spoke loudly, urgently, shouting something to me and the healer. The medical Mage looked up in confusion, but it was too late.

Darkness took me.

The first thing I noticed when I woke was the voices. They were loud, near-shouting, and whatever they were saying had to be up-setting in some way as they talked very quickly. I couldn't quite make out whatever it was, my head pounding whenever I tried to focus. *Could they be quiet for just a moment?*

They, quite obviously, could not hear my silent complaints as whoever it was continued their loud discussion. One of the voices was familiar to me, though I couldn't figure out why. Seeing no way for me to continue my rest, I decided to open my eyes and figure out what all the fuss was about and why it had to happen inside my room as I slept. *Did Tristifer forget to lock the door again?*

Opening my eyes with some difficulty, the lids felt as if they were made from stone, I squinted as the sudden brightness of the room hit me. Too bright to be my room, in fact. Far, far too bright. I could make out two shapes in the brightness, one wearing red and the other blue, standing out clearly in a sea of white. "W-where...?"

The two figures turned to look in my direction, and I heard something that sounded distinctly like "Richard" come from the one on the right. The one in red. The blue-garbed one moved to grab something I couldn't quite make out yet from beside him, but it looked like a drink of some sort. As the red figure continued to speak muffled words to me, the blue gently lifted my head up and pressed something cool to my lips. A drink, like I thought.

Herbal – bitter and earthy. Disgusting. Medicine?

Slowly it all came back to me as the medicine passed my lips. My disappointment in the coursework, complaining to the Grand Master, studying Conjuration at the library and my first attempts at it before finally remembering the pawprints. I sat up suddenly, ignoring the burning in my chest and stomach as my body screamed in protest.

"Grand Master! I need to see the Grand Master!" The blue figure, one of the school's healers, I recalled, attempted to stop me and hold me down. However, they were far weaker than the one that had pinned me before. The room became clearer as my panic sharpened my senses and I saw that I was in one of the medical wards, the pure white walls and flooring making it quite clear. The healer in question was a young man with a darker skin tone, like those in the southern portions of the Kingdom. Outside of the frustrated glare he was giving me for my resistance, I thought he looked quite comely and kind.

"Yes, yes you do, Richard. We have much to discuss, I suspect." Turning, I looked at the red-garbed individual and saw them clearly for the first time. The Grand Master was not pleased, his eyes holding me in place. "Leave us, Healer Byron"

"Sir, I still think this is a bad idea. His condition is still..." Whatever the healer made to say was cut off as the Grand Master's eyes moved to him, pinning him with the same sharp and steely look. "Yes, sir. Just please make sure he doesn't leave the bed."

The idea of being alone with the Grand Master right now was not an appealing one, and I almost begged the man to stay. But I know he couldn't defy the man's orders. He was the supreme authority on the campus, after all. No one wanted to be on his bad side. Well, outside Professor Daylin, perhaps. So, I staid quiet as the kindly looking healer departed the room, noting with of annoyance that he also locked the door.

"Richard...What happened?" The Grand Master said, starting right to the point as soon as we were alone. I turned to see the older man staring at me with the same steel-eyed expression, mouth set in a firm line of disapproval. "Did you *summon* something? I saw the prints."

I winced at the question. Summoning something without a supervisor, specifically one approved by the school, was out of the question for students. Too many had called upon a beast, or entity in the worst cases, that they couldn't handle. The destruction and death had been catastrophic, according to records. "Not...exactly, sir."

I could almost see the older man's mind working quickly, even without me having to tell him the full details. He knew what I had been studying and, based on our conversation in his office all those weeks ago, knew that I am someone that wants to go above and beyond the norm. Still, I decided to speak and admit what he had already likely figured out. "Conjuration. I...Conjured something."

Grimacing, the Grand Master closed his eyes and exhaled deeply. His hands clasping together tightly as he sat in silence and I knew he was waiting for more information. So, I continued to speak. I explained what I had conjured, that I had not seen any records of similar events in the past and I thought that it would impress both my peers and the teachers at the university. Maybe even earning me my Mastery without the exam. Throughout my quick explanation, summarizing my time in the library and studying, to my thoughts about conjuring animals, the man did not speak or open his eyes. It wasn't until the very end, when I reached my meek admission about the warding and what had occurred with them, and my cutting them both, that he reacted.

Turning away from me so suddenly that I nearly jumped, the Grand Master shook his head slowly. His hand reaching up to rub his head as he thought over what I had said. Finally, he turned, and I found myself unable to tear myself away from his harsh glare.

"You're not the first." He said, holding me in place with his eyes.

It took me a moment to realize what he'd said, and I furrowed my brow in confusion. "I saw no other records of living conjuration, Sir. Not in any of the books that I found available at the library..."

"Because all records of those incidents had been *purged* for a reason! Conjuring non-living materials and items is hard enough for the unskilled, and those that attempt what you did normally don't *survive* their first mistake to make a second!" He roared at me, and I felt myself snap at the harsh treatment.

"How was I supposed to know what would happen? There are no warnings in the books, no records to serve as a cautionary tale, nothing! For all I knew, I was entering uncharted territory! Besides, the damned thing is gone now, right? You saw the prints!" At the mention of the prints, we both paled a little. The changes in them, the monstrosity they appeared to morph into, flashed in my mind. I quickly forced the thoughts away and took a breath to calm myself. I and saw him do the same.

"No. No it is not gone, Richard. And I fear it won't leave any time soon. Not until it finishes what it started." The anger bled from the man and he sighed deeply, moving to sit at the foot of my hospital bed. "Do you know *why* living conjuration isn't done?"

The question threw me off guard at first, but I recovered quickly. As drained and foggy as my mind was, I could still recall the events that transpired prior to me awakening in the medical ward. The power drain had been immense, as had the concentration needed. Not only that, but even one mistake, such as my attention slipping, should have been the end of the caster. I relayed my thoughts to the older Mage.

"Well, yes, but no." Shaking his head, the Grand Master takes a moment to formulate his answer. Looking to the ceiling in thought before turning to focus on me. "While it is true that the concentration and power needed are immense, and a single mistake can be costly, the real danger is what happens if something *does* form out of it. Tell me – where does magic come from?"

"Either from ourselves or the world around us, depending on the nature of the spell and its weave. Are you saying that the leopard doesn't have a source of magic?" I considered that line of thought, struggling to understand it. "That it's a spell without, what, a power source?"

"Exactly. Every living thing, whether it can access it or not, has some form of magical energy. Life energy if you will. It is utilized on a day to day basis, source that wanes and grows, replenishes, and diminishes, as we go about our lives. However, a spell does not have this property. It has what it is. Your creation is the same. It does not have a source and every moment of its existence drains what energy it has." At the end of the pseudo lecture, I felt I had a better understanding of what the man was trying to convey.

The leopard, or whatever it was now, was, in essence, a living spell. When it had been conjured, I had poured a not-so-insignificant amount of energy into it. For a normal spell, the amount of magical energy would have lasted days, but for a conjured creature, who consumed magic with every thought, movement, etcetera, it should be running on empty or approaching it any moment now. Even if you take into consideration the vast amount that had likely been transferred by the nature siphoning wards.

"Doesn't that mean that it will disappear soon, Sir? It's been several hours since you found me." I shivered slightly, remembering the state I'd been in. "The magic has to be running out."

The man shook his head slowly, staring at me with a mix of pity and anger. "No, Richard. Perhaps had you not attempted to stop the wards in the way that you had that might be true, but not anymore."

"Sir? What do you mean?" I felt my unease grow and a weight landed in my stomach. *What does that mean? I cut the wards and the spell stopped siphoning from them, right? Wait...it was still attached to me – to my magic! Is there something wrong with my magic?!*

Panicking, I reached inward to the well of power that resided inside of me and was horrified by what I found. My terror must have been clearly visible as the Grand Master only nodded and placed a comforting hand on my shoulder. He attempted to speak to me, to comfort me no doubt, but I failed to hear any of the man's words. My mind focused on what I felt deep inside of me.

If you were to take the average Mage and describe the power that they could draw upon, you would not be incorrect to compare it to the size of your average pond. Large enough to do just about all your low to mid-tier magics, if they diligently studied and learned to control it. However, certain Mages had far larger and deeper reserves to draw on. Using the same analogy, it would be like a lake, of varying size and depth depending on the individual. I fell into one second category, and I was not bragging when I said I had an impressively vast and deep lake of power to draw upon.

So, you can imagine my shock, and horror, when I reached into my being and found not a lake, drained and a little battered from my recent actions, but a small pond. A ridiculously small pond. Miniscule. I wasn't even sure I could call myself a Mage anymore. I tore my gaze from inward to grab at the Grand Master's hand, shaking and scrambling, trying to understand.

"It's gone! Sir, what happened? Who did this?! Where did it go?!" I screamed, clawing at the beddings that covered me in hysterics. I tried to toss the blanket off me, to rise up, to do *something*.

The Grand Master's strong hands clasped my shoulder and my arm, preventing me from moving. He shoved me back into the bed, roughly, and I could barely make out the sounds of him dismissing the medical Mages that had entered the room at the sounds of my duress. My heart pounded in my ears, drowning out all other sounds, and my breath came in short, shallow, gasps.

A rough smack to the side of my head drew my attention and pulled me from my hysteria, forcing my attention back to the man in front of me. I rubbed the struck area, the pain a needed distraction from my panic. Seeing that he had my attention, the Grand Master nodded and gestured up and down at me.

"This is exactly what I mean. Everything has a price, Richard. This is especially true for magic, something *you* should be aware of. In your haste to stop the spell and the wards feeding it, you provided the weave an incomplete magical core to rely on – crippling your own in the process. This allows the creature *you* brought into the world to survive far longer than it otherwise should, though at a price." The unease reappeared in force, and I lifted my gaze up from my hands to meet his solemn one.

"A price, Sir? What do you mean?" I asked, afraid of the answer.

"Your core and this creature are now linked together, but only yours can be refilled naturally. It will feed, finding sources of magic to empower itself and prolong its life – something it will no doubt find in abundance here. Regardless, the fact remains that it is incomplete. It will come for you to finish the job." The older man said without pity, and his words had my entire body stiffening in fear. He nodded slowly at me, and I could see he was pleased I saw the horror in what he said. "Yes, Mr. Foxx. In your attempt to prove your superiority, rushing blindly and thoughtlessly ahead, you have endangered yourself and everyone at this school."

CHAPTER 7

"How do we stop it?!" I asked before I could stop myself. The older man looked surprised at the question but shook his head after a moment of consideration.

"I do not know. And even if I did, you are in no condition to do anything." His words made me pause and for a moment I was confused, as I was not severely injured.

Not physically, maybe... The thought caused me to wince outwardly, something the Grand Master nodded grimly at. The reminder of my greatly diminished power had me laying back in the bed with a sigh. "...Will I ever recover?"

"Perhaps with time, or perhaps with the death of this creature. In truth, Richard, I do not have the answer to that question, either. Your magic may return to you with its death, or..." He trailed off, not voicing the thoughts that I had begun to consider.

If the Beast died, would it take my power with it? What would become of me? Not just magically, but in terms of my enrollment here. I had broken likely dozens of rules. Knowingly or not, and I was still angry about the lack of information that was clearly need-to-know, I had endangered the school. There would be consequences, I'm sure. I decided to voice my concerns to the Grand Master.

"Sir, what will become of me?" My question had his brows raising, and he lifted his hand to his chin in consideration.

"We – the teachers and I – have not yet decided. Likely, however, your time at this institute will be over once this crisis is resolved." There was no doubt in his voice that would be the result. The idea of leaving this school as a disgrace, maybe even a prisoner, filled me with despair. *What would my father think? What would Tristifer?*

I don't know why I was concerned with the opinion of my roommate, but the thought of his view of me souring was disheartening. My father would be gratified, I think. He always believed nothing good would come of studying here. It looks like he was right. *I attempted to prove myself and now others will suffer for my own selfishness.*

"What if I killed the Beast myself?" I asked on impulse. The question caught the older man off guard, and he leaned back in his chair. Placing his hands on his lap and shaking his head at me.

"Mr. Foxx. Richard. You're simply not strong enough now. Even discounting your current state, the magical drain you have suffered recently is more than enough to..." The Grand Master began, eyebrows raising in surprise.

"What if, Grand Master? Please." I interrupted. I like to think that I didn't beg, but I know I came close. The tone appeared to have an effect as the older Mage sighed deeply and rubbed his brow.

"You would still be punished, but expulsion...Perhaps a case could be made to avoid it. Suspension, a hold, perhaps permanent, on any Masteries for years, if not decades. Regardless, this is on the assumption that you *could* kill such a Beast as you are now." He said, raising a good point. However, we both knew this conversation was pointless, and I decided to end it by stating what we had been avoiding.

"You said yourself, Sir. This creature will come for me. It's not a matter of *if*, but *when*. Why not take the fight to it?" I dreaded facing whatever my would-be leopard had become, but I knew it was only a matter of time before I had to. "We've wasted too much time already. We need to plan, to act. To hunt and destroy it."

"Rest assured, Mr. Foxx, we've not been idle the few hours you've been asleep. I've had teachers patrolling the grounds since you pointed out the prints to me and have evacuated the school of all non-essential personnel. The only reason you are still here is my belief that whatever you unleashed would return to finish what was started." The Grand Master stood, moving to look out the blinds of a nearby window.

"So, what? I'm the bait?" I couldn't hide the disbelief in my voice. "You're using me as a piece of meat, hoping the beast comes for a bite!"

"You just stated you wanted to help moments ago, didn't you? The only difference between then and now is that you're a *willing* piece of meat." The Mage shrugged and closed the blinds, looking back at me. "Rest up well, Mr. Foxx. I have a feeling that the night will be a long one…"

With that, he moved to the door and, with a glance back at me, exited the room. A medical Mage entering soon after to look me over. He was not happy about the situation, and I suspect the Grand Master would have complaints cross his desk soon, but he did his duty. Checking me for any abnormalities, outside my decimated magic levels, and gave me a few potions before exiting the way he had come. Leaving me utterly alone.

Duty. The word left a sour taste in my mouth. *Righting my wrongs. How can I kill this Beast as I am now?*

Despite the Grand Master's words, I found myself unable to get any rest. The thought of what was out there, waiting, hunting, had me staring at the window in uncertainty. Watching every shadow with apprehension.

The sound opening of my door being thrown open had me jolting awake and scrambling, turning to face the entrance as my heart hammered in my chest. I released a breath I didn't know I was holding when I noticed it was the Grand Master, who hurried inside. I was confused when didn't shut the door behind him. A quick glance at a clock on the wall made me realize that it had been near two hours since our last conversation.

"Sir?" I questioned, rubbing the sleep from my eyes.

"We need to move to a more secure location." As he spoke, he moved. Tossing what I absently noted to be my cloak towards me. A pair of shoes were hastily placed on the floor beside my bed as

I struggled to slip on the fabric. I nearly question where all the clothes had come from but stopped when I saw his expression.

The sight of his pale skin and the barely hidden fear in his eyes was all it took for me to snap awake and obey his unspoken instructions. I quickly moved to leave my bed on shaking legs, almost falling as they struggled to support my weight. Slipping on my shoes and tightening their strings, I finished placing the cloak over the thin clothes the healers had provided me. Looking around, I noted that the Grand Master was back at the door, whispering to another figure I couldn't see clearly. I moved to the doorway on shaking legs, squinting to make out the other individual and was shocked at who I saw.

Professor Aleric? I could barely make out the man's shaved head, something only two teachers at the university had, and one was not nearly so tall, or a man. Regardless, seeing the professor of Battle Magic eased some of the fear that filled me. Despite our poor relation, I would admit freely that the man was competent.

"Richard, come. Aleric, you have the lead." The Grand Master said, seeing that I was standing and making my way over. He looked at my shaking legs and grimaced. A gesture that I shared with him. *I'm going to slow them down. I'm going to put them in even more danger.*

"You sure about this, Ulirk? It's a long run – walk." Aleric corrected himself, glancing down at my legs. The man didn't look at my face, and I could feel the disdain he felt for me. More than my duel in the courtyard and reading in his class would warrant. The Grand Master must have shared the truth with him, then. What I had done. *How many more know?*

"I'll be fine, Sirs. I'll keep up. Where are we going? What's going on?" Moving to the two men as confidently and swiftly as I could.

"The Vault. Professor Daylin is dead – drained dry." The words had me stumbling, and I grabbed at the door frame for support.

The Grand Master looked pained at the words he spoke, even if Professor Daylin had been a life-long rival of his. Perhaps because she had been, even. They had known each other since their school days, after all. *Wait, drained? Don't tell me…*

DAWN'S ARRIVAL

"What do you mean, "drained dry?!" My mind whirled at the words, still fighting off the grogginess of sleep. Slowly, I recalled the Grand Master's words about the leopard – the Beast.

"Your little experiment has fed, Mr. Foxx. And its fed quite well. You're no longer safe here." It was Aleric that spoke. His dark brown eyes, nearly black I noted absent-mindedly, burning into me.

The rest of the conversation prior to me falling asleep came rushing back to me and my eyes widened. "I thought the plan was to hunt it, using me as bait?"

It was to the Grand Master that I directed this question, but before the man could answer, Aleric cut in. "We don't have time to discuss your would-be plans. We have to move, now."

As the bald Mage spoke, he began to do just that. Heading down the hallway without waiting for us. We hurried to follow, my weakened state slowing me down more than I would have liked. Every dozen or so feet felt like a hundred, and a brisk walking pace felt like a jog. Still, I did my best to keep up. The Grand Master staying just ahead of me and glancing back to ensure that it stayed that way.

The halls were empty, save for the decorations and doors leading to other rooms, similar to the one I had been in. Thankfully, the magic torches functioned fine, keeping us illuminated and able to navigate without worry. Still, the lack of any other personnel, medical Mage or otherwise, left me feeling wary.

"Sir? Where is everyone? The teachers and school security, I mean. There are others, right?" My question didn't slow the man, and he answered without looking back at me.

"Outside, Mr. Foxx. They're waiting to escort you to The Vault." I nodded, not that he could see it, and we turned left as we came up to the floor's reception area. Aleric quickly glanced down the center of the staircase that lay just ahead and nodded at something, or someone I assume, below. He turned to the Grand Master and I and motioned us forward, keeping his eyes behind us.

The idea of steps, especially in my current condition, was not appealing. Sadly, there was no other way. I doubt Aleric would be willing to wait for one of the magic lifts in the building. So, with a muttered curse, I moved passed the two men and took the steps as swiftly as I could. At the base of the staircase I noted an individual that I wasn't familiar with, He was younger than both Aleric and the Grand Master by several years and possessing bright red hair. *An assistant?*

My thoughts were interrupted as the gleaming head of Professor Aleric moved in front of me, followed by the greying hair of the Grand Master. They shared a glance at me, then Aleric motioned to my right, towards the rear entrance of the medical ward. I absently noted that that entrance was also the furthest from Professor Daylin's office in the Alchemy ward, which was located just left of the building we were in.

"I'll take lead again, Ulirk, you're in the rear. Kain keep to the left of Mr. Foxx." Aleric's voice broke me from my thoughts, and I nodded in understanding. Moving to follow the man as he cautiously began to lead down the well-lit halls. I heard the Grand Master fall in behind me as the assistant, Kain, took his position to my left. The young man didn't seem to understand what was happening, I think. He wasn't shooting me glares of disgust or mistrust, for one, and I think he even looked confused.

*Stupid not to tell him, but at least I can trust him to not toss me to the Beast...*Keeping my eyes forward, but my ears open, I followed the shining head of Aleric down the halls.

As we moved, I could not help but feel something...wrong with the situation. A feeling that had me stopping abruptly only a few meters from where we had started, causing both Kain and the Grand Master to stop short. The older man nearly stumbling into me, letting out a curse. Cautiously, I glanced around us, noting that Aleric hadn't stopped moving. "Professor?"

"Hm? Mr. Foxx, we don't have time. We have to keep moving!" Aleric said turning to look at us. His mouth thinning in anger as he gestured for us to follow him. "We're nearly at the door!"

"Professor, I don't think we should go that way." I said, softly. Looking behind him to the doorway. The unease growing the more I looked at it. "Let's use the side exit."

"What? No! Too risky." Aleric shook his gleaming head. Pointing over his shoulder towards our original destination. "Everyone's waiting for us out there – it's the safest way."

"It doesn't…feel right. It feels like somethings waiting out there." At my words, the Grand Master looked up, startled. Moving passed me, I noted the stirrings of magic in the air with some relief. At least my senses hadn't been affected by my loss of power. Though, they were weaker, not as precise. I debated on activating The Sight to see more clearly but decided against it.

"…Aleric, let us use the side entrance. It's not that far a walk, we can signal the others to meet us there." The Grand Master said, and I noticed his eyes moving along patterns that I couldn't see. Again, I was tempted to use my Sight, just to see what he does, but the remembrance of my drained and depleted core stopped me. *I hate being unable to do anything…*

"Sir? What do you see?" The older Mage didn't answer, but whatever it was he had seen affected him deeply. I could see the deep sadness in his face, and the start of tears.

Aleric, having heard the Grand Master's words, and my question, turned to look at the doorway himself, utilizing the Sight himself while doing so. Slowly, he began to back away. A look of confusion crossing his face. "…Daylin? No…It can't be."

At his words, my eyes snapped to the door and I began to back away. Slowly at first, but faster and faster. Kain, unaware of the situation, only looked on in confusion as the three of us quickly began to backtrack beyond the foot of the staircase. The young assistant turned to look towards the door in question and squinted.

"Daylin? Professor Daylin? I don't see her out there. Sirs? What's going…on…" The young man's words slowed, and he began to falter in his speech as a shadow moved just beyond the doorway. The darkness outside providing the perfect shield and the light from the magic torches creating a glare that made it near impossible to see. "Hello? Who's there?!"

"Kain! Move, now! Get over here!" Aleric yelled, but it was too late.

The moment that the young assistant yelled to the shadowy figure, demanding its identity, it moved quickly. Faster than anything so large should be able to. One moment, it was hidden behind the cover of glare and glass, and the next, the shadow was inside, shattering through the thin barrier without pause. It decided upon the poor man with a roar, half man and half beast, tearing into the assistant before he had the chance to so much as whimper.

Finally, I saw what it was that I had unleashed. There was almost no resemblance to the leopard I had attempted to conjure. No spotted pelt, elegant short muzzle, or trim and fit body. Instead, it was an ugly, towering thing, easily twice my height and thrice as broad. Made entirely of muscle and what fur it had left was matted, falling from it in clumps as its flesh rippled like water. Its arms and legs, still somewhat animal like, ended in the massive talons I recalled the prints in my room morphing into. Even without my Sight I could see the currents of magic rushing through its moving flesh. Bright flashes of color under angry red muscle. The Beast looked like it was ready to burst apart at any moment. *By the Gods, what have I created?*

"Richard! Richard, run!" The Grand Master's voice broke me from my horror, and I turned to look at the two men that had been escorting me. They were a dozen feet or more away, near the hallway that led to a side entrance, exit in this case, and gesturing me to hurry.

I didn't need any more encouragement than that. Turning away from the horror behind me, I sprinted towards them with all the haste I could muster. I heard the beast's talons scraping the stone floor as it moved. A sharp, ear piercing sound that had me clutching at my head in pain, followed by a wet splattering noise as it dropped what was likely Kain's corpse. I could see the horror on the face of the Grand Master as he turned to flee towards the exit, Aleric having already left both of us behind.

As I turned a corner and ran down the short hallway, I heard the beast begin to move. Its large form shaking the very ground beneath my feet as it thundered towards us – towards me. I didn't need the Sight to know its body was empowered by the magics it had drained from both Professor Daylin and poor Kain, providing it with speed and power. I barely managed to slip through the ancient doors of the medical ward before Aleric and the Grand Master slammed them shut. The reinforced wood buckling from the impact of the creature that had been at my heels. My heart hammered at the speed that the Beast had closed the distance, and how near I had been to death.

"That won't hold for long! We have to get to The Vault! Signal the others!" The Grand Master said, shaking me to bring my focus back. Nodding to Aleric, the older Mage grabbed me by the arm and pulled me with him as he sprinted away from the medical ward.

"We won't make it – it's too fast!" I said as I followed the man as best as I could, stumbling as he practically dragged me across the courtyard. "We need to slow it down. Reinforce the door, create additional barriers of stone, anything!"

"That won't stop it. It eats magic, Mr. Foxx. We have to assume this means all forms of magic." The Grand Master said as a bright flash of red light filled the night sky – the signal to the other professors and school personnel. "Spells and Enchantments, even from the inorganic."

"The Vault is our only option, then?" I winced as the beast slammed into the doors far behind us, roaring as it attempted to brute force its way through them. "Isn't it magically reinforced? Won't that just make it stronger?"

"It's also has thick steel walls – the thickest available to us." The sound of hurried footsteps on stone had the older Mage glancing over his shoulder. I didn't need to look to know that Professor Aleric had rejoined us.

"I sent the signal but didn't receive any in response. Ulirk, I think that maybe…" Whatever the Battle Magics professor was going to say was cut off as the beast's roars, which had been loud but distant, suddenly increased dramatically in sound.

Immediately after we heard the strain of wood, creaking and groaning as it attempted to contain our, my, hunter before, suddenly and violently, the barrier gave. The ancient, iron reinforced doors bursting outward into fragments and splinters as the massive monstrosity broke through them. Smashing through them with such force that it appeared to surprise even itself, its form scrambling to maintain its balance as it was flung into the stone courtyard. Its talons scraping across stone in that horrible, glass-shattering, manner.

"Inside! Quickly!" The Grand Master said, turning to the first building available. He didn't bother finding a key, simply blasting through the door with a burst of magic power and sending the barrier flying into the hall behind in splinters.

We rushed through the newly created opening as the Beast finished collecting itself, roaring in what I could only assume was rage and hunger. The pounding of its gargantuan, taloned, fists thundering behind us as we fled down the darkened halls of what I absently remembered being the Charms and Enchanting building. As we ran down the hall we could hear the shatter of the stone and wooden door frame behind us, the Beast having burst through the opening with far greater ease than it had the reinforced doors of the medical ward. The shattered frame and bits of stone showering the wall across from the ruined entrance way as the creature forced itself through the too-small passage.

It was bigger now than before, Kain's magic having fed it further. I could see it swelling even as it rampaged towards us, filling the hall with its mass more and more, pushing the walls outward. Its neck, or whatever that mass of coiled magic-filled muscle was, was extending as it hungrily opened and closed its mouth towards us. Drool slicking the floor behind it like slime.

"We need to slow it down!" Aleric said, flicking his hand behind him as we ran. The stone floor rising to create a wall that connected to the ceiling above. "Even if the damn thing sucks the magic out of it, it's still going to at least buy us time!"

And make it stronger! I wanted to say but didn't. The bald Mage was right. We needed every second more than we needed magic at this moment.

Something the Grand Master seemed to agree with as he joined the Battle Magic professor in creating wall after wall of stone between us and the Beast. We could hear the enraged calls of the magical abomination as it encountered the first layer of defenses. The shattering of stone rang out over and over as it brought them down without pause. Soon, the Grand Master and Aleric were creating barriers that were twice, even thrice, as thick as those that came before them. The sounds of shattering stone became slower, with more time between, and I caught a glimpse of a side passage that I frequently used.

"Grand Master! Professor! There!" I quickly made my way over, gesturing for the two men to follow me. "This way!"

At first, they appeared confused why I would want to use this passage, but it soon became clear to them as they sprinted over. It was far smaller than the main walkway that we had been backpedaling in. Maybe just large enough for two men to stand comfortably side by side, but no bigger. They both exchanged nods and pushed me into it, with Aleric quickly turning to the way we had come and summoned forth yet another wall. This one far thicker than any before it. *It must be at least two feet thick, maybe more – far too big to break!*

"Good thinking, lad. It'll have a hard time following us through here." The Grand Master said, quickly making his way down the passage. "This leads to the library, doesn't it?"

"Yes, I took this path quite often." I said, sprinting after the man, or as close to a sprint as I could. The fear and panic had dulled my sense of pain for a time, but it had begun to return. And two-fold. "The Vault isn't far from it, right?"

"The library's too big, cutting through it won't work. The Beast will have too much room to move." Aleric wiped at his brow and dabbed at his head with a handkerchief.

"Aye, but it might be our only option. The only other building in the area is the Combat Magic ward, and you know those walls are magically reinforced." The Grand Master said, leading the two of us quickly down the cramped passage before taking a left for several paces, then a right. Behind us the Beast could be heard roaring as it attempted to bash its way through the stone wall that had been hastily created. Each impact shaking the building around us. "We cannot allow it to grow any stronger."

I saw Aleric look at me from the corner of his eye, glancing me up and down to take in my current state. I knew I looked how I felt. Exhausted, pained, and terrified out of my mind. I was running on fumes, and he could see it. The bald Mage slowly shook his head and turned back to the Grand Master.

"Ulirk, we can't keep this up. Mr. Foxx – Richard – is half dead on his feet already, and that thing is coming no matter what we put in its path. We need a plan, an *actual* plan. Not run and hide and wait for help." The Grand Master stopped, just for a moment, but continued to move as another impact shook the building. It was harder, stronger, this time. The Beast was no doubt feeding on the wall.

"I know, Aleric. Help's not coming. I knew the moment you signaled for the others and they never came." It didn't take me longer than a second to understand the implications of his words. Once I did, I felt the world fall out from underneath me.

"You mean…?" I questioned, swallowing hard when the two men nodded. The building shook again as the Beast slammed its now considerable mass against the stone barrier far behind us. "Then how do we stop it?! What can possibly kill it now?!"

"We need to get to The Vault." The Grand Master said again, stopping to turn and look at us both. "It is the *only* way."

Aleric and I could only nod in agreement, following the greying Mage as he led us further down the passage and toward the exit. Behind us the Beast roared, and the building trembled. The thick stone wall all that separated it from us. We quickly made our way out the old wooden door at the end of the passage and closed it hard behind.

CHAPTER 8

Making our way across the courtyard and towards the library, the three of us didn't bother with stealth. Sprinting at full speed towards the towering building, or as much of a sprint as we could. We were all slowed due to our varying levels of exhaustion, though I knew both men would refuse to admit their condition. I could tell from the sweat on the Grand Master's brow as well as both his and Aleric's labored breaths that they had been drained by keeping the Beast at bay.

"We don't stop! Cut through the library and out the other end, The Vault is just beyond it!" The Grand Master declared, pointing to the wide double doors of the building in question.

"Wait – do you hear that?" Aleric suddenly said, looking towards the Charms ward behind us. The Grand Master and I slowed to listen but did not stop. What we heard, or did not hear, in this case, had us sprinting again with Aleric following close behind.

The loud, thunderous, impacts of the Beast on the wall behind us had ceased. Either it had busted through the stone barrier, unlikely given that it wasn't charging out the door behind us, or it had gone around it. In either case, it was coming, and we didn't have time to waste. I reached the doors seconds before the other two men and pulled hard, feeling a rush of panic when they didn't budge.

"They're locked!" Both men cursed and moved me aside to try themselves, finding that I spoke true. Aleric kicking the door in frustration and looking around us.

"We'll have to go around." The bald Mage said, starting to move away. The Grand Master grabbed his arm before he could get too far, shaking his head frantically.

"No, Aleric. It is too dangerous. Look." The greying man gestured in the opposite direction that Aleric had been to moving in. The Combat Magic professor and I followed his finger towards the street in question.

In our haste to open the door, we must have missed it. The magic torches had gone out in the left side of the courtyard and beyond. The pathway, which would have led directly to The Vault, was nearly pitch black. A far cry from how I distinctly remember it being when we had exited the Charms ward.

"We need to get indoors, Grand Master." I said, keeping my voice low and nervously looked around us. The flickering of light in the corner of my vision drew my attention, and I turned quickly to see the torches on the other end of the street, opposite the ones that had already been extinguished, fading. "We need to get indoors *now*."

"The doors and locks are made from a special material – they resist magic. We'd need the key." The Grand Master tried the doors again, shaking his head and giving the reinforced wooden barrier a kick as Aleric had. "We'll have to find another way."

Turning back towards the now dimly lit area, the only light coming from two torches positioned on either side of the library doors, we considered our options. The library was vast and nearly at the center of the Old Campus. On either side of it were streets, the now shadowy and unlit areas that Aleric had been about to make his way into. There were several small buildings around the massive structure, including both the Combat Magic and Medical wards, as well as a small storage building to the left of the library. As far as I recalled, the storage building has no rear exit.

"We cannot go back the way we came, and the Combat Magic ward cannot be risked." The Grand Master turned back to the locked doors of the library. "This is the only way. Aleric, keep watch! Foxx, stay close!"

Holding his hand out to his side, the greying Mage furrowed his brow in concentration. It took only a moment for me to realize what he was doing – Conjuration. The Grand Master was Conjuring something into his hand! *I didn't know – when? How? I should have asked him for help!*

As quickly as the thought had come, I dismissed it and shook my head. I had disregarded any ideas of seeking help because I was afraid they would stop me, after all. A fear that, in hindsight, I should have paid more attention to. Dropping the revelation that he *could* Conjure, I instead focused on what he *would.*

Perhaps a key? If he knows what the library key looks like then – no, wait. It's resistant to magic. It would fall apart the moment it entered the lock. Or at least it would in theory. The key would be a purely magical item, after all.

I received the answer to my question as a hatchet appeared in the hand of the older man. I looked at him in disbelief. "Are you serious? It's going to take time to…"

My protests were cut short as he handed the axe to me and set about forming another for himself. "Me?! Sir, I'm hardly in any shape to be swinging an *axe!*"

Catching a heavy object with a grunt, having conjured a larger, two-handed felling axe for himself, the Grand Master turned to look at me seriously. "Then we do it together. Tell me, Mr. Foxx – do you want to die tonight? No? Then start swinging."

He accented his point by bringing his axe down into the reinforced door, cutting into the barrier with grunt of rage and desperation. His strike was near the handle of the left door, and I immediately understood his plan. Bringing back my axe to strike when he pulled away, I bit back a curse as the impact raddled my wrist. The moment I pulled back to swing again, his axe came down, striking where I had just hit. A pattern quickly took shape, fueled by our desperation and fear.

The sudden flickering of light to our sides had us pausing, and we looked up to see the magically powered torches on either side of the library's entrance dimming slowly. The Grand Master's eyes flickered, and I saw the signs of the Sight being used. Against my better judgement, and likely any rational thought, I decided to risk using it myself, unwilling to hold back my curiosity any longer. My considerably drained pool of magic felt awkward to use, but I cautiously dipped into it and turned my gaze upward. Following a small trail of power being tugged in that direction. My heart stopped at the sight that greeted me and the hatchet nearly fell from my hands.

If the Beast had been horrible to behold before, it was truly an abomination now. While there had been some remnants of what it was meant to have been in its appearance, small tufts of fur and a semi-feline head, there was nothing of that in the unnatural monstrosity that it had become. Already barely contained mutations had grown wildly out of control and the power that it had devoured so greedily only further caused its physical form to distort and change.

The Beast's arms were long now, double the length of its torso, and large with muscle. Hands, talons, more like, clutched at the roof top of the library with a powerful grip. Its nails puncturing through the stone surface with ease. The lower body was unseen to me, but I could make out the shadows of appendages moving in the dim light of the moon. I thought they looked similar to the illustrations of squids and other sea beasts described by sailors in old tales. All of this paled in comparison to what had happened to its face. Or rather, *faces* now.

There was nothing left of a leopard in *either* of its two monstrous faces. A wide, gaping maw situated in the center of a massive torso drooled and gurgled fresh blood, no doubt from those that had come to assist us, ran from its fang-filled maw. At the top of this torso was a long, almost tube-like, neck that ended in a lamprey-like head. The beginnings of which I had seen forming in the Charms ward when the neck had been extending. The lamprey's mouth was where the magic of the torches was drawn to, sucked into its tooth-filled circular maw.

"Dear Gods…" I heard the Grand Master mutter.

"They had nothing to do with this…" Aleric said in response, and I felt his gaze on me. It was at this moment that I felt myself snap. In fear, self-loathing, or a combination of both, I wasn't sure. All that mattered is that energy filled me, and I moved.

Tearing my gaze from the monster that was perched just above us, I started to attack the door with more ferocity than before. The memory of the Beast fresh in my mind as the lights began to dim more and more, driving me to move faster and faster. The Grand Master, seeing my panicked pace, worked with me. Hammering his axe into the door blindly, not just at the handle like myself. Suddenly, with a cracking sound, the head of my hatchet went further forward than I had anticipated, throwing me off balance and into the door. My head hit the wooden barrier hard, and I lost my grip on the handle of the axe.

Panicking, and disorientated, I attempted to grab at the tool, reaching down to catch it as it fell – only for it to fall forwards, following the head. I faintly heard it clatter to the floor, muffled by the wooden barrier. Shaking my head and leaning back I felt relief fill me at the sight of a hole near the door's handle.

"Grand Master!" I alerted the man, who had already moved before I had the time to speak. He must have heard the hatchet fall and guessed what had occurred.

Nodding sharply as he reached into the hole, pushing me to the side, the Grand Master grit his teeth when he was jabbed by the wood. It was just barely wide enough for his hand and part of his arm, but it was enough. Reaching inside of the hole, I saw, and heard, him muttering curses as he moved his hand inside near the door handle. Suddenly, a loud clicking noise was heard. The door was unlocked, we'd done it.

It was at that moment that the faint light of the torches finally dissipated entirely, leaving us in darkness. My eyes snapped to the roof and I squinted to see anything using the dim light of the moon. I could barely make out the Beast perched above us searching, moving its massive form from side to side on the edge of the roof, driven by what I knew was an endless hunger for magic. A part of me hoped that there was some torch that hadn't been touched yet, or maybe that the Best would go for the Combat Magic to drain its magically reinforced walls, but that hope was dashed when it leaned forward. The hungry maw in its torso growling, drooling profusely. The lamprey-like head locked onto Aleric, the bald Mage being furthest from the doors.

"We need to move, now!" I yelled, moving to grab the Grand Master's hand and rip it from the door, throwing one half of the barrier open. Ignoring the shout of pain from the older man, I shoved him inside and quickly followed him in. Turning to yell for the Aleric to follow us, I found the words getting caught in my throat as a large shadow moved in the air above us.

The Beast descended quickly and without warning, slamming into the stairs leading to the library with such force that it cracked the smooth stone and shattered both sides of the railing. It happened so fast that Aleric was completely caught off guard, and I could see the man attempt to scream before the mouth of the lamprey latched on to him. Its tooth-filled maw covering his entire head in one smooth motion, sinking down to his neck. The massive arms of the Beast grabbed the legs of the doomed Mage guided them down to the mouth in its torso. Aleric's screams were muffle, as said mouth bit down on the limbs, soon over-shadowed by the crack of bones and splattering of blood. The crimson liquid now running down the broken stone steps, staining white marble red. I could myself unable to look away as the Beast devoured Aleric quickly, its two torsos making short work of his flesh – and magic.

The door was slammed in front of me just as the lamprey mouth began to pull, and Aleric's own neck began to follow suit. Separating from his body, which was quickly consumed by the Beast's torso-mouth. I tore my gaze from the door, the horror I witnessed still fresh in my mind, and looked the Grand Master in the eyes. His ashen face covered in sweat as he gestured for me to get away from the barrier.

I could only obey, stumbling away from the massive doors as the man set to work securing it with whatever means he could, magical or otherwise. As the greying Mage raised thick stone walls in haste, ripping the materials needed through the wooden floors and up from the very foundation of the building, I doubled over and lost what little food I had in my stomach.

When will this horrible night end? Even through the door I could hear the snapping of bones and wet splats of blood and flesh hitting stone as the beast feasted on Aleric. Each sound making my stomach churn as I fought the urge to vomit again. Suddenly, the noise stopped, and we heard the Beast begin to move. It paced for a moment outside the door before, suddenly, moving away. Its massive form shaking the ground, letting us track its position.

"It's...going around the library." The Grand Master said, and I nodded in response. Drawing myself up to my full height and gesturing to the other end of the massive room, past the Lorekeeper's circle of desks. The man paled when he followed my finger, bursting into action and rushing forward.

At the *unbarricaded* wooden doors. The Library's other entrance.

CHAPTER 9

"We need to seal the doors." The Grand Master said, rushing to the other end of the library Following the man, looking at the Lorekeeper's workstation as we passed, I couldn't help but think of how drastically life had changed since the last time I was here.

"Wouldn't that trap us here, Sir?" I asked, switching to a jog to keep up with the older man, ignoring my aching muscles. "I thought we were going to The Vault?"

"Yes. Yes, it would. Do you honestly think we would make it, Mr. Foxx? Should we step outside?" The question caught me off-guard, but I thought back to Aleric's fate. I quickly drew the same conclusion as the older man.

"No. We wouldn't stand a chance." Drawing close to the doors, the greying Mage quickly set about barricading the wooden barriers as best as he could. The strain it placed on him was easily visible, and I doubted even his considerable magic reserves would last much longer.

He's an Elemental Magics user and hasn't actively taught a class in years. This must be wearing on him. Magic was, at times, like a muscle. You could over focus on certain aspects, like speed or endurance, and weaken yourself in others. Especially if you didn't use it often. *I wish I could help in* some *way!*

Watching the older mage work, the Grand Master finished not a moment too soon as right when he finished raising a stone barrier, the frame shook. Shuddering from the impact of something large, and powerful, striking it. The Beast roared, angered at being denied its next meal, and stomped around the exterior of the building. Testing the door again and again with its considerable weight and strength. Thankfully, the walls, frame, and stone barrier held. For the moment. My eyes caught sight of the stained-glass windows and I felt a flash of worry but pushed it down for now. The creature doesn't appear to know about them, yet. *We're lucky it doesn't seem too bright.*

"We can't remain here, Sir. We have to kill it." I said, looking to the Grand Master as he took a seat. The older man was panting from the exertion, likely due to the many barriers he'd had to form in such a small period.

"I know, Mr. Foxx. I know. I had hoped to find a way to do so in The Vault, but that path is now blocked to us." Wiping his brown, he frowned and took a deep breath as he leaned against the door to one of the library's many small study rooms.

"I've studied many of the objects on display there, Sir, none of them would have been able to assist us. They're all magical in nature. I'm surprised the Beast hasn't made its way over there to devour them, in fact." Taking a seat across from the man, I winced at yet another impact on the door, this one stronger than the others. A cracking sound told me that the wooden door had broken, but the stone barrier held strong.

"Yes, the artifacts we *allow* students to see. There are others located deeper in The Vault. More secretive and far more powerful. It is not these objects that I wanted to access, however. There are tomes and records, too." I caught the meaning of his words immediately, sitting up straighter.

"Including on the last instances of conjuring the living." At the man's nod, I saw his plan more clearly. He had hoped to find a way to undo the spell keeping the Beast alive. "But that option is now closed to us, now. There's nothing left."

At my words, the man's face darkened, and he shook his head. I felt a familiar unease fill me at his face as he looked me up and down. Finally, he spoke, and his words did little to alleviate my feelings. "It is, yes. But it was not the only option. There is another."

"Then why haven't we taken it?! If you knew a way to kill the Beast, why haven't you done so?!" I leapt to my feet, glaring down at the man. My unease having replaced by rage, the memory of Kain and Aleric's ends fresh in my mind.

"Because, Mr. Foxx, I did not, and still do not, believe it to be viable." The Grand Master spoke, calmly, holding my glare without flinching. His grey eyes staring into my brown without a hint of fear. In fact, I could see only contempt, disgust, in them.

This contempt, the hatred and disgust I could see in the older Mage's eyes, killed the fire that raged in my chest. The idea that the man I had admired, and still do admire, would see me in such a light…It hurt. Far more than the many aches and pains I had accumulated in the last few hours. So, anger snuffed out, I sank down to the floor and looked at my lap. Taking a moment to compose myself before speaking again.

"Tell me what you know, Sir. Please." The Beast smashed into the stone barrier again, and I heard the shattered remnants of the door be flung into the street at the impact. The stone wall shuddered, and I swore I heard a cracking sound, but did not give. We both waited, breath held, but it appeared the most recent impact had stunned the monster and it didn't strike again.

"This creature, Mr. Foxx, is linked to your very essence. You are part of it, and it is a part of you. Your magic gave it life, and your core was consumed to sustain it. You're a bright lad – I'm sure you understand the implications." The Grand Master said, and though his words were spoken softly, I could hear the underlining rage. I ignored it, however, and pressed him further.

"Why didn't you kill me, then? Or have Aleric, or the others, do it?" I asked, softly, keeping my gaze on my lap. Slowly starting to understand what he was saying. "Why does it want to kill me if my being alive is what sustains it? Wouldn't killing me be killing itself?"

"No. Killing you wouldn't kill the Beast. It would merely continue feasting without end until either it was put down, or there was nothing magical left to devour." Shaking his head, the Grand Master gestured to the stone barrier, wincing as it shook again. The creature having recovered, I guessed. "It needs you. It cannot end its hunger without you. Your core, your very essence, is needed to *complete* it."

The stone wall cracked from the next blow it took, the strength and size of the creature finally taking its toll. I had no doubt that the magic used in creating the stone barrier had long been drained, too. Simple stone would not last much longer against such an onslaught. We were running out of time and the Grand Master's resigned face told me he knew that, too.

"How, then? How do I kill it?" I asked. My voice was quiet, and my heart hammered in fear. Part of me knew already, but I needed to hear it. I needed to hear him say it.

"We, you, poison your magic core. And you let it devour you. Poison your core so thoroughly that you become the very Void itself." My spine stiffed as if iron had replaced it, and I lifted my gaze to meet his grey one. "You must undo what you've done – restore balance."

"You're asking me to...destroy myself." There was no other term for it. This wasn't suicide, this was annihilation. I would be nothing – there would be nothing left. No soul, no magic, no trace of my existence except a mangled corpse. "Surely there's another way!"

"There isn't. And that is why I didn't tell you. You, who are so selfish, so proud and arrogant. You would never make the choice. No matter what was at stake." I flinched at the man's contempt, his voice hard and dripping with venom. Sadly, he was right.

It had been my pride that had led us to this point. My belief that I could do anything, even something as complicated insane as conjuring a living being. I had called it *easy*. Worst of all, I had done it to impress others and showcase my superiority. In doing so I had caused the deaths of dozens of Mages tonight.

A familiar sensation filled me, and I lifted my head to meet the golden eyes of Drakari, the wolf-God staring down at me from the painted-glass windows above. As he had done so many times leading up to this moment. Part of me, a more superstitious part, whispered that the mortal-turned-God had obviously known. He had seen this coming and tried to warn me, tried to tell me that I was making a mistake. The signs had been there. The unease, the doubt, and the many warnings I had gotten about going too far, too fast. But I knew the truth. I knew that was me searching for a scapegoat. Part of me wanted to blame the Gods for this nightmare, but that would have been childish.

This nightmare has nothing to do with the Gods. It was my fault, and I should do my duty to make it right. Struggling to my feet, hissing through clenched teeth as the pain hit me, I nodded down to the Grand Master. Laughing slightly at his confused face.

"You're right. That *is* who I am. Arrogant, proud. Selfish. I'm sorry, Sir." Moving slowly, ignoring the aching in my muscles and bones, I made my way to the barrier that separated us from the monster that I had created. The stone shuddering from yet another impact.

"What are you doing, Mr. Foxx?!" Shouted the older Mage, and I felt his disbelieving gaze bore into my back.

"Being selfish, Sir! Only one of us gets to kill this beast, and that's me!" I said, giving a half-smile over my shoulder at the man before turning back to the slightly cracked stone. *Because it's my duty.*

Ignoring my own fears and doubts, and the voice that cried for me to flee upstairs and hide, a tempting proposition, I opened my Sight and looked deep into myself. To the diminished pond that was now my magic core. My very soul. The energy quivered at my mind's touch, as if it sensed what I intended to do, but it did not resist me. Pushing against it, I forced my consciousness into the pool of power and sank deep. Deep into its very depths, towards the bottom. I needed to create a void, a hungry, insatiable maelstrom that would consume me and anything linked to me. But I couldn't do it just yet.

Opening my eyes, I turned my attention to the stone wall and waited, watching as the cracks grew larger and more prominent from every impact. I could see, out of the corner of my eye, that the Grand Master was moving towards a staircase, seeking higher ground to hide. I didn't blame him. A large part of me still screaming at me to do the same. Still, I held firm.

Finally, with an explosion of stone and a roar of anger, the

Beast tore through the barrier and forced itself into the doorway of the library. The compact frame unable to contain its mass as it was broken inwards. My body was pelted with shards of stone and wood, several of which cut me deeply and caused me to bite my lip in pain. Still, I did not run or turn away. For the first time since the Medical ward, I came face to face with the abomination that I had created. Fear filled me, fear of both the Beast and of what I was about to do. But, most of all, I felt...sorrow.

"I'm sorry." Looking at the mutated, horrifying, form of what could have been a beautiful creature, I could not help but be filled with regret. Regret for the mockery of life that I had given it. Death at the hands of The Void would be a far better fate. "Don't worry. I'll make things right."

The words didn't have any impact on the Beast, of course, and its lamprey head looked about the library, searching for anything to devour. Finally, it locked on to me and perked up in a way that I hadn't when it had seen Aleric. A result of our linked cores I suspect. It rushed towards me, smashing through anything in its way and sending shards of stone flying in all directions. I braced myself for the pain and heard the shout of the Grand Master as the Beast gripped me in its massive talons.

It was then, at this moment, as I saw the lamprey-like head descending towards me, that I reached deep into my core and pulled at the seams that bound it together. Shredding them with a viciousness that surprised even me. The pain was excruciating and, for a moment, surpassed anything that the Beast could do to me. I felt my very essence be ripped from me, torn into oblivion as The Void filled me up, shredding mind and soul to nothing. My last thoughts were of a smiling blond, holding out his hand and a proposition I wish, desperately, I had accepted.

EPILOGUE

It took me hours to make my way down from the second floor of the now ruined library. The Beast had destroyed the staircase in its last death-throws, and my exhaustion had made it difficult, if not impossible, to get to the ground floor with a spell. As I reached the lower level, I took in the shattered remains of the once-great center of learning. My heart ached for the loss of knowledge.

"The night took a heavy toll..." I muttered, making my way through the rubble, searching. Running a hand through my greying hair, I knew that it would likely grow much whiter after the last few hours.

Spotting the massive corpse of the creature in the far corner of the room, having nearly broken through the library's wall during its last moments, I shuddered. The Beast had died in agony, both of its mouths screaming in a dozen voices as it perished. The hunger that had driven it up to the point of its death amplified a thousand-fold as its false magic core rotted. It had taken half an hour for the abomination to finally die of starvation.

"A fitting end." Glaring at the corpse as I walked, I grimaced as I finally came across what I had been searching for. It was a gruesome sight, like many I had experienced in the last few hours.

Removing my cloak, I knelt and, after a moment's pause, covered the mangled corpse. There was not much left of the young man, having been half-devoured by the time his last act had taken root. Placing a hand on the cloak after a moment, I sighed in regret.

"You were right, Mr. Foxx. You were selfish" I had grossly misjudged Richard. In the end, he had done the right thing. Even knowing full well what would happen to him. "But I was wrong about you. I'm sorry."

Drawing myself up to my full height with a groan, I slowly made my way towards the entrance of the library. Taking care to avoid falling as I crossed the shattered remains of the stone wall I had risen to hold the beast at bay I paused to examine the library's entryway. The doorway would need to be completely reconstructed, as would much of the campus I suspect, but it, and the school, would survive. *The nightmare is finally over.*

"Grand Master! Grand Master!" Ripping my attention from the ruined doorway, I moved out of the library fully to find the source of the voice. Another survivor, a young woman. She was beaten and bruised, briskly walking with a slight limp, but alive. She was just as surprised to see me, given her face, especially when she looked at where I had come from.

"I'm glad to see someone else survived. Are there any others with you?" She smiled and nodded, gesturing behind her.

"Some. We took refuge in the Combat Magic ward." I stiffened and stared at her in shock and partial disbelief. "What? It had reinforced walls, seemed like the perfect place. Though, it looks like whatever it was focused on the library. I guess you already knew that."

*Ah, they must not have known about the Beast's magic-eating properties...*Recovering from the shock that there had been a small group of survivors not 100 meters from us, I collected myself and nodded. Gesturing to the ruined doorway behind me and clearing my throat.

"Aye, it did. It chased Richard Foxx, Professor Aleric, and I for most of the night." I noticed her eyes widen at the second name, and absent-mindedly recalled that she was Aleric's assistant. It pained me to break the news to her. "I'm sorry to say that they did not survive the night."

"Oh." Her expression fell, and she looked to the ground. I tried to find the words to comfort her but couldn't. I hadn't known the man well, despite being colleagues for years. A moment later, her gaze lifted, and she cleared her throat. "What of the creature?"

"Dead as well. It was actually Mr. Foxx that had killed it." The memory of the young man's death flashed in my mind. "Though at a great cost."

"He's a hero, then." She said, nodding her head in relief as she looked to the rising sun. The relief on her exhausted face clear to see.

I began to respond in the contrary but paused in consideration. I could tell her, tell the world, the truth of the Beast. That Richard Foxx had caused the nightmare we endured to begin with, a fact that only the senior professors had been aware of. Something that only I knew now, it appeared. *But...*

Turning to look over my shoulder at the ruined entryway to the library, spotting the corner of the tattered cloak I had lain over Richard's body. I couldn't help the half-smile that formed on my face, both proud and sad. *Perhaps, in his own way...*

"...Yes, he was." I agreed with her. Turning to face dawn's arrival with the young assistant and placing a hand on her shoulder in comfort, I closed my eyes and enjoyed the warmth of the sun. "A hero indeed."

Printed in Great Britain
by Amazon

DAWN'S ARRIVAL

Cody Ragland

Cover and illustration design by: @GrizzKeltz

I would like to thank my family and friends for pushing me and encouraging me to write and pursue my dreams. This book would not have been possible without your continued support and I am deeply humbled by your love everyday.

A special thanks in particular to my friend @GrizzKeltz for doing the art in this book.